A Fool and Her Honey

A Fool and Her Honey

Kimberly T. Matthews

www.urbanbooks.net

Urban Books, LLC
78 East Industry Court
Deer Park, NY 11729

ISBN 13: 978-1-60162-382-9
ISBN 10: 1-60162-382-8

First Trade Paperback Printing April 2013
Printed in the United States of America

10 9 8 7 6 5 4 3 2 1

This is a work of fiction. Any references or similarities to actual events, real people, living or dead, or to real locales are intended to give the novel a sense of reality. Any similarity in other names, characters, places, and incidents is entirely coincidental.

Distributed by Kensington Publishing Corp.
Submit Wholesale Orders to:
Kensington Publishing Corp.
C/O Penguin Group (USA) Inc.
Attention: Order Processing
405 Murray Hill Parkway
East Rutherford, NJ 07073-2316
Phone: 1-800-526-0275
Fax: 1-800-227-9604

A Fool and Her Honey

Kimberly T. Matthews

Chapter 1

Candis

Give me a head full of curly hair and call me Joan Clayton from *Girlfriends,* because I was pretty desperate for a man. I came to this realization a few weeks ago as I was sitting at my desk, browsing through a thousand e-mails, sipping a cup of made-at-home gourmet coffee, and reviewing my priorities calendar. I was supposed to be designing and sending out my electronic invitation for my thirtieth birthday bash, coming up in just four short weeks, but I got sidetracked when I realized I'd be entering my thirties without a love interest. Yeah. I was about to say good-bye to my twenties and greet the big three-o, and I just knew I'd have a steady man in my life by now.

Every single birthday for the past eight years, I'd spent with my girls Celeste and Dina. There is nothing like being celebrated by your best friends on your day, but just once I'd like to spend it being romanced by a man who actually loved me. Hell, at this point, I'd settle for one who just liked me a lot. Unfortunately, this year looked like it would be like all the years that had come before it. Hot lovemaking and cuddling substituted for the buzzing sound of a battery-operated adult toy.

"Oh well, maybe next year," I sighed as I reached for my vibrating phone, already knowing it was Dina calling to see if I'd still make our weekly brunch. "Hey, girl."

"Hey. You are still coming, right?"

Dina knew me well. I had a habit of burying myself in my photography work and forsaking my friends. I'd always have good intentions of going, but more often than not, something would prevent me from following through, something like, I just didn't feel like getting dressed. "Yep, I'll be there."

"You always say that, Candis. I already talked to Celeste, and she's coming, so you better come," she chided.

"Dina, I'm going to be there," I replied, committing myself again. Honestly, I could use some time with my girlfriends after the week I'd had. I finally decided to completely break it off with Russell about a month before, and I was currently suffering through withdrawals.

The last night Russell and I were together was simply for convenient sex. After he left, I must have cried for about an hour. I was feeling empty, defeated, useless, and unhappy because, overall, the relationship was completely unfulfilling. Actually, Russell was probably quite content, but our relationship left a lot to be desired as far as I was concerned. Did I not deserve happiness and success? I wasn't one to embrace karma, per se, but I'd heard forever that you reaped what you sowed, and God didn't like ugly. So I had to wonder, what had I done so ugly in my life that God was getting me back with a string of relationship failures?

Okay, there was that one time that I slept with Cynthia Parkinson's husband. And by one time, I mean I'd messed with somebody's husband only one time. Chad and I had a full-blown affair that lasted more than a year. Yeah, I fell for that typical stuff men say when they are trying to land an extra piece of ass instead of going home to their wives:

"She doesn't pay me any attention."

"She's not attentive to my needs."

"We are having problems and are about to divorce."

"We're together only for the kids' sake."

"We're separated right now."

I believed every word of it, and before I could stop myself, I was pulling down my panties for Chad on the regular and waiting for him to leave his wife.

Then it didn't help that sex with Chad was some of the best sex I had ever had in my life. And I had had quite a few lovers that I could compare him to. Chad had me sprung. He was sensitive and skillful; he stayed tuned in to my reactions to his touch, his kiss, his speed and his stroke. Chad loved me up so good that just the thought of him made me run to get my Silver Bullet toy. I even showed him how to use it on me once, and like an honor roll student, he mastered it in a snap and combined it with his own tricks and turned me out something terrible. Sex that good was hard to come by, so I had to wonder what the hell was wrong with his wife that she couldn't get her act together and keep her man happy. If I were Chad's wife, I'd be doing whatever he wanted me to do all day, every day.

Feeling guilty but believing his lies, I did try to hold out to become Chad's new wife. With the way he was coming over to my place all the time and rolling around in my bed, it was like we were married. I convinced myself that they had to be separated, because what wife wouldn't have a whole lot to say about her husband being gone all the time? Wouldn't she eventually follow him or have him followed to find out what the hell was going on with her missing man? During the time that we dated, that man brought me flowers, told me I was beautiful, and gave me all kinds of gifts, from jewelry to furniture to cold, hard cash to line the inside of my purse. And did I mention the sex?

It was all good, until his wife found out and showed up at my door one day, looking for a fight. Even if I hadn't been caught off guard, I could barely stomp a spider without running scared, so fighting someone was out of the question. She beat my ass good. Hair snatched out, eye blackened, lip busted up, earring yanked out—all of that. I'd never been so humiliated in my life. And even with that said, I couldn't even blame the woman. I had it coming. I was screwing her man, I knew it, and I knew better. Needless to say, I never gave Chad another thought after that, even after he left me a million voice-mail apologies and came over multiple times, ringing the doorbell until I thought it would fall off the frame of the house. Wasn't that much good sex in the world to take another beat down like his wife gave me that day.

I was grateful that she used only her fists and feet, instead of showing up with a gun or crowbar. I swore off dating after that, while I tried to get myself together both physically and mentally. I was scared for a long time, not knowing if Cynthia was satisfied with the punishment she'd given me, or if I'd be out shopping somewhere or, God forbid, meeting a client, and she would decide that what she gave me wasn't good enough. My worst nightmare was to have her pop out of the bushes and go whaling on me all over again. I did think about pressing charges, but I couldn't do that in good conscience, knowing the damage I'd done to her marriage and probably to her self-esteem.

I did take some safety measures, though. Right away I had a security system installed at my home and my photography studio, and I looked into some martial-arts-based self-defense classes. I never did go to them. Owning a gun, even if it was only to fire a warning shot into the air to scare her if I needed to, seemed like a better use of my time and money.

Anyway, like I said, after that fiasco I swore off dating altogether for a long while. It just wasn't worth the drama to me. And as long as I kept a few batteries around the house, I was able to take the edge off of my private sexual tension. If I ran out of good batteries, I knew how to use my fingers. But real talk, a toy, and a finger wiggle were no substitute for a nice, thick, warm-blooded man, and I got tired of lying up in my bed with a buzzer all the time. We all want someone to love us and love on us, right? I didn't know a single person who didn't appreciate the words of the late Teddy Pendergrass: "It's so good lovin' somebody and somebody loves you back." Which was what I'd been hoping for when I met Russell, but that turned out to be a waste of my time and my emotions.

I had to come up with a better strategy for getting and keeping a real man. Maybe if I would just pray about it, God would have somebody in mind that He wouldn't mind hooking me up with. If anybody knew about a good man, He did. And I had to have asked God to forgive me for the whole Chad thing at least one hundred times. So was it that He didn't hear me or He didn't forgive me? Or was it that I just never took the time to ask Him to give me a man who was tailor made for me? And how many times had I heard that He could do the impossible, or that nothing was impossible with Him? Lots of times.

I knew He still made good men who were capable of loving a woman, because look at Dina's man, Bertrand. If there had ever been such a thing as a man in love, Bertrand was the perfect example. With a smile as wide as the ocean, he said he fell in love with Dina at first sight, and all Dina had been doing was standing in line at the post office to get a book of stamps. He saw her, he approached her, he swept her clean off her feet, and he proposed to her in less than six months' time.

Had he not come along, I didn't know if I would have thought that men like that were still out there. To date, none of them had ever come my way, that was for damn sure. I was almost convinced that attached somewhere to my body was a sign visible only to the most doggish of men that read FOR A GOOD TIME, STOP HERE. Every last one of my relationships involved a man who was absolutely no good for me, but I was always too foolish to see it, giving them my all and getting almost nothing in return.

I couldn't take another year of this mess. Obviously, I didn't know how to pick a man, so why not let God do it for me? He orchestrated a couple of hookups in the Bible, didn't He? Well, if He did it for others, He could do it for me. With nothing to lose, I decided to ask Him.

I'll make a deal with you, God. I'll go to church, and you bring me a good man. One that loves you and will love me the way I need to be loved. Deal?

All right. Now let's see what happens.

Chapter 2

Candis

Dina had been worrying me to death about visiting her church with her, and since I'd made this deal with the Lord, I decided to go with her one Sunday and see what good picks were available in the congregation where she worshipped. Who knows? I might just meet Mr. Right.

I slipped into a white maxi dress that had large, bold red, orange, and yellow flowers and paired it with a matching shrug. My French pedicure still looked pretty fresh, although it had been weeks since I'd gotten my feet done, so I strapped on a pair of red four-inch sandals. I kept my makeup to a minimum because in the heat of the day, it did nothing but slide off my face. A little mascara to make my eyes pop, a little gloss so my lips did the same, and a little bronzer so I looked gently kissed by the sun, and I was ready to go.

I pulled up to her church about ten minutes before the service was scheduled to start, found a seat midway in the sanctuary, one not too close but not too far from anyone, then sent Dina a text.

> Where are you?
> I'm in the lobby. You here?
> Yeah. I'm sitting in middle section, kinda close to the front.
> K. On my way.

Dina didn't reach me until just before the praise and worship part of the service started, which required everyone to stand.

"What's wrong with you?" I asked. Dina was looking a little crazy in the face.

"Nothing. Just had a stressful morning," she answered with a quick shake of her head. "I'm fine."

I didn't believe her, because almost as soon as the people on the stage, altar, or platform, or whatever it was called in church, started singing, Dina began to cry. Her tears started off slowly but were soon traveling rapidly down her face, even though she tried to hold it together. Her shoulders were trembling as she kept gasping and sniffing into a wad of tissue handed to her by a passing usher. Whatever it was, she was pretty torn up about it, but I let her cry in peace and not gawk at her and force her to tell me what was going on.

I was trying to concentrate on the words, the music, and the worship. I couldn't quite get my mind on that particular track with Dina quietly sobbing on one side of me and my thoughts circling around who I could possibly find as a suitable mate. My eyes kept scanning for available men, even though I tried to stop myself at least four times. Shameful, I knew, but it was what it was.

They sang maybe three songs, then went through announcements and a welcome that required me to stand unwillingly again to be acknowledged as a first-time visitor. During this time, Dina seemed to pull herself together, but she was still looking right sad. I wanted to pinch her on the leg for all this standing up and carrying on, but I had to remember my deal with God. I didn't want to give Him any reason to renege.

It wasn't until the choir was preparing to sing that I saw a gentleman who caught my eye. He stepped to the front of the choir, picked up a microphone, and flashed a smile that was worthy of magazine print. He was dressed in charcoal-gray slacks, a slate-blue shirt, and a tie that blended well with both.

"Praise the Lord, everybody!" he yelled, to which the congregation mumbled a response, repeating his words. He said it twice more, and the congregation grew louder with their response each time. "I'm a little nervous this morning, but He's still worthy, amen."

"That's all right, baby," a woman replied from behind me.

I leaned over and whispered to Dina, "Who is that?"

"His name is Hamilton Taylor."

Hamilton. Hmm. Nice.

Hamilton opened his mouth and let out a singing voice so soulfully beautiful, it gave me goose bumps.

"Take my heart and mold it. Take my mind, transform it. Take my will, conform it to yours, to yours, oh, Lord!" he sang with his eyes tightly closed and his brows scrunched down over his eyelids. He sounded amazing.

"You better sing, Hamm!" Dina shouted beside me, clapping her hands wildly. "That boy can sing!"

I felt like I was in the Eddie Murphy movie *Coming to America,* in the scene where the three men were listening to the group Sexual Chocolate botch Whitney Houston's "The Greatest Love of All." It made me laugh out loud, but the difference was that Hamilton, Hamm—whatever his name was—really could sing, and I was moved and impressed. When the song ended, about two thousand people were standing up all over the sanctuary, clapping, crying, holding up their hands, and waving their arms in the air, along with shouting words of praise.

"So what's his deal?" I whispered to Dina as most people were getting resettled in their respective seats. A few remained standing and carrying on.

"I'll tell you later," she blurted under her breath.

I didn't know if that meant something bad or if she just didn't want to be bothered right now. I decided to assume it was the latter, and because I was anxious to hear all about him, or whatever Dina knew, the service seemed excessively long. Finally, the last amen was said. I grabbed my purse and followed Dina toward the door, ready to get outside and hear what she had to say about Hamilton. Instead of her beating a path to the exit, Dina stopped along the way to hug and say hello to what seemed like every single person there.

"I'll meet you at the house," I interjected between her chitchatty lines with another woman about an up-coming women's conference. I made my way through a mini throng of people, some moving, others standing and talking, and finally reached the foyer. Much to my surprise and luck, Hamilton was standing by one of the exits, handing out some kind of flyer to passersby. I eased my way over there pretending that my only intention was to leave the building.

"How're you doing, sis?" he said, pushing a flyer my way.

"Good, thank you. What's this?"

"Oh, we're having a community day the Saturday after next, and we need a few more volunteers. You were one of the first-time visitors, right?" he asked while others rushed past me, grabbing flyers from him, patting him on the back, and speaking a few words.

"Yeah," I answered, half looking at him and half reading the flyer.

"Well, thank you for visiting us. How'd you enjoy the service?"

"It was great." Then I looked at him directly. "I really enjoyed your song. You have a beautiful voice."

"Thank you, sis. It's nothing," he said, looking bashful.

"No, it was awesome," I replied, complementing him further.

"Well, thank you."

"I'm going to have to see what I have on the calendar for this day," I commented, holding my now rolled-up flyer in my hand. "It would be nice to give back to the community."

"Yeah. We can use all the help we can get. If you have any questions about it, feel free to give me a call at the number that's up there."

I thanked him again and almost skipped to my car, impressed with how fast God worked. Premature excitement, I knew, but what was wrong with that?

Brunch was at my house, so I rushed home to make Mediterranean chicken wraps, cut up some fresh fruit, and prepare mimosas for us ladies. I broiled hot dogs and set out chips and lemonade for the kiddies. I had a few board games to keep them occupied, as well, but normally Celeste's boys kept themselves occupied with handheld video game systems.

I hoped Dina would be in a talking mood once she got to my house so she could tell me a little more about Hamilton.

"Slow your roll, homegirl," I coached myself out loud, knowing how quickly in the past I had thrown myself wholeheartedly into a relationship mess. "Don't be so quick to take a dive."

"So, Dina, give me the rundown on Hamilton." I couldn't help myself. I attacked her as soon as she stepped both feet inside my condo.

"What do you want to know?" she answered, then immediately turned her attention to her cell phone, having received a text that obviously required her immediate attention. She was silent for several seconds as her thumbs went to work on a response, but she didn't circle back around to what I'd asked once she dropped her phone in her purse. "Lawd! These shoes were killing me today. Woo-weee!"

I waited for her to get back to me after she eased her feet out of her heels and wiggled her toes, but she acted like I hadn't asked anything at all. *Let me give it a few minutes,* I thought. Maybe she needed to get some food in her system to get her brain cells going.

"This chicken wrap is so good, girl. What all is in it?" She stuffed her mouth with another bite, then jumped up from the table and flew to the door, stating that she needed to get somebody's phone number from her car.

One thing that irritated me about Dina was she knew how to be conveniently distracted to keep from answering questions. I could give her church and worship time, but now that we were sitting at my dining room table and she didn't have tears rolling down her face, I expected her to start talking.

"Dina, stop ignoring me," I practically whined when she returned from her car.

"Ignoring you about what?" she asked, thumbing through her phone. "Oh, let me text Sister Edmonds while my mind is on it."

Oh, now her ass had forgotten. Dina could be really self-absorbed sometimes. Whatever. I'd just find out for myself.

Chapter 3

Celeste

Believe it or not, the best part of my day was getting out of my own home and going to work just so I could get away from my husband for eight hours, and I didn't even like my job that much. The best part of his day was probably seeing me leave, because he'd have the next eight hours to do what he did best when he was between jobs—absolutely nothing. That was how it had been for every single year of our marriage. Maybe I could make it through one more day.

With a sigh, I sat up and planted my feet on the floor. I was about to get up for the day, leaving Equanto on his side of the bed, snoring as usual. I had only a few minutes to myself in the bathroom to take care of my personal business and get dressed before I'd have the kids on my heels with their daily breakfast, getting dressed, and their school drop-off routine. If I expected to enjoy my cup of coffee in peace this morning, I needed to hustle.

Before I stood up, I reached toward the foot of the bed, grabbed my robe, slipped my arms into the sleeves, and pulled it around my body. I didn't want Equanto to crack his eyes and catch sight of my almost naked body on my way to the bathroom. Every time he saw me even partially undressed, he would make some kind of comment in reference to my weight, not to mention the faces he made when he saw me butt-bald naked.

I knew I needed to lose some weight, and by some, I meant at least one hundred pounds, as my current weight was right at two fifty-six. That was what having babies could do to a woman. That, and my worst catch-22 ever, which was when I didn't feel good about my weight, I got depressed, and when I got depressed, I ate a lot. Then, when I ate a lot, I gained weight, and when I gained weight, I didn't feel good about it.

It wasn't like I didn't try to control it; I did. Seemed like every other day, I was trying to be on a diet: a restriction diet, calorie counting, the watermelon diet, the no-carbs diet, the rice diet, Atkins, Jenny Craig, the Master Cleanse, HCG drops. You name it, I'd tried it at least for a day or two, but I'd never been successful, because I just loved good food. I loved the way it tasted and how it felt in my mouth. It was comforting to me when my world was in disarray, which was most of the time.

Nothing made me feel as good as a great plate of food: some fried chicken, candied yams, butter beans with bacon cooked in, homemade macaroni and cheese, corn bread, buttery biscuits, coconut cake, deep fried pies, chocolate chip cookies. . . . I could go on forever. A few pieces of carrot and a handful of grapes with a boiled egg and a cup of yogurt didn't do a thing for me but make me cranky and irritable. I had enough drama going on in my home without me contributing to it with rabbit-style eating habits.

To make sure my day was off to a good start, I planned to cook the kids homemade waffles topped with strawberry preserves, scrambled eggs with cheese, and sausage. The kind that came in a plastic roll and had to be formed into patties by hand, then fried up in a pan. Lawd, that was some good eating right there! I hurried through my shower to give me enough time to cook before I had to get the kids on the school bus.

It took about ten minutes of quick cooking to create an aroma powerful enough to call my boys out of their sleep. Linwood padded into the kitchen first, rubbing his eyes.

"Good morning, Mommy," he mumbled, throwing his arms around my waist when he reached me.

"Good morning, baby. You hungry?"

"Yes. I was dreaming that I was eating pancakes, and then I woke up."

"How about waffles instead?"

"Yummy!" He smiled, looking over at the waffle maker to check the ready light indicator. "Is it ready yet?"

"Go wash your face and brush your teeth and wake your brothers up. Then you can eat."

Once the three of them, Linwood, Quincy, and Jerrod, were seated and eating, I rushed to my bedroom and pulled on a pair of elastic-waist black pants and a camisole, curled my hair, and threw on some makeup. My favorite royal blue blouse was laid out on the back of a chair today. The office staff at the realty company I worked at as an admin had to take new badge pictures, and the blouse went well with my skin tone and made me look radiant . . . and not so big, which was good for photos.

"You make me a plate?" Equanto asked, still reclining in bed but reaching over to the nightstand to get the TV remote.

Oh God, he was up.

"No, but there's some in there on the stove when you get ready to eat," I answered, not looking at him, but instead pulling at my eyes to apply my eyeliner.

"Okay, I'm ready to eat now."

"Great. The kitchen is in the same place as it was last night when you went to bed, E. I know you remember where it is."

"So you can't serve your man?"

"Are you going to get the kids dressed?"

"How long is it gonna take you to put some food on a plate and bring it in here?" he asked, disregarding my question.

"It'll take me no time today, because I'm not going to do it."

"See? That's messed up right there."

"Yeah, whatever." I walked out of the bedroom to tend to the children, leaving him mumbling words that I'd rather not hear under his breath. I'd heard them all before, anyway. He was just calling me names, and I didn't have time to get my emotions all worked up this morning.

While I dressed the kids, Equanto yelled from the bedroom, "I'm 'bout to get dressed and I'ma need the car today, so don't leave me. I'll drop you off at work."

"What do you need the car for, Equanto?"

"I got some things to do today," he said, appearing in the doorway of the boys' room, bare-chested and in his boxers.

"Like what?"

I already knew that he had nothing to do but wreak havoc on our lives, both mine and his own. We'd been through this type of thing a million times before. Whenever he needed to use the car, something crazy would happen. Crazy like one time he'd been on the way to give the landlord the rent money. He stopped by the convenience store to get a soda and left the money on the front seat of the car, because he forgot about it. When he came back out, the money was gone. Crazy like as soon as he cashed his check, some dudes came up to the car while he was at a traffic light, held a gun to his head, and demanded his wallet Then they took all the money out and threw the wallet back in the car, hitting him in the face with it. Crazy like he made a mistake and left the front door unlocked when he went to the grocery store. When he came back, someone had come in the house and had taken all the boys' video games but had left the rest of the house intact. Hell, no, he wasn't getting the car.

"I need to go check on this job one of my boys told me about that pays more money than the one I was trying to get."

"Just call them, because you're not getting this car."

"Call them?" He crinkled his brows. "Don't nobody be taking job applications over the phone no more."

"Well, I don't know what you're gonna do, then." I shrugged, pushing past him to put my blouse on and complete my look. The two minutes it took me to put on my blouse and throw on some accessories were the same two minutes it took my husband to grab and hide my keys and my cell phone. He watched me circle the house, turning stuff upside down in a complete panic, having a cussin', screaming fit for twenty minutes, while he lay back on the bed, watching BET.

"I gotta go to work, E. Stop playing!" I was on my last and final leg at work for being late and having to miss work, and I was in no position to lose my job.

"Ain't nobody playing. Get your ass out there and catch the bus if you gotta leave."

"You know damn well that's gonna make me late for work!" If I didn't get out of that house in the next two minutes, I'd never make it to downtown Phoenix in time for work.

"I told you, I don't know what you did with them."

"It's not about what I did with them. It's what *you* did with them."

"I ain't had 'em," he lied.

I knew he was lying, and it didn't take me long to become frustrated and angry and to burst into tears. I called Candis, hoping her day wasn't jam-packed with appointments. She heard how upset I was, so I didn't have to say much to get her to pick me and the kids up willingly, drop me off at work, and take my boys to school, but by the time I got to work, it was too late. I'd already been written up quite a few times for being late, and most of the time it was for this same type of mess, and by me being late and not calling, my boss had no more tolerance. He had termination papers waiting on me when I got there, forty-five minutes past my scheduled start time.

I didn't call Candis back for a ride a second time. I cried first as I walked to the bus stop. Then, instead of going home, where I wasn't sure that I'd be able to control my emotions enough to keep from killing my husband, I took the bus that would drop me off near Golden Corral.

Chapter 4

Candis

Hamilton was the first person I looked for when I got to the church grounds that Saturday, pretending to be interested in the community outreach function. I couldn't have cared less, actually, but whatever would bring me closer to getting to know Hamilton, I was willing to do. Dina and I got there early enough to help set up some tents and booths and hang out some clothes that were being sold. I made myself busy with those tasks until finally, the man I hoped to get a little face time with drove up in a late-model silver Mercedes and parked in the lot.

He stepped out, looking as gorgeous as a Hawaiian sunset, dressed in tan khaki cargo shorts, a dark blue polo shirt, and a matching pair of canvas deck shoes. His calves, shoulders, and forearms bulged with muscles that bragged of his apparent workout schedule. I tried not to stare the man down, but I couldn't help myself. Every time I tried looking away, my eyes found their way right back to wherever he was.

Hamilton soon joined a few other brothers, slapping hands with them and sharing a casual chuckle, then helping them clear a path for the car wash, which would be adjacent to where the yard sale tables had been positioned. Wanting to make sure that I wouldn't be assigned to a place farther away from him, like the hot dog stand or the kiddie area, I found the biggest box of miscellaneous items that I could and offered to sort, price, and set them out on tables.

"Chile, thank you so much, 'cause I shole didn't wanna be the one to have to go through this stuff," said the older woman who was heading up the yard sale section.

"Whatever I can do to help." *And get next to Hamilton.* "I don't mind at all."

Now, I didn't throw myself at the man's feet, but from behind my shades, I treated myself to a glance every chance I got as I placed things on various tables, trying to think up a way either to get him to notice me or to approach him and not seem too obvious. I couldn't go ask him anything, because our workstations were too different and it just didn't make sense. The only thing I could think of was to "make a mistake" and knock a table over. With that in mind, I went to work placing items on four different tables, one for knickknacks, one for books, tapes, CDs, and DVDs, one for dishes, and one for pots and pans, which would be my "turnover" table. The only thing was it took me close to an hour to get my stunt set up, and by the time I did, I was as sweaty as a hound dog and tired of digging through boxes of other people's gently used trash.

I wished I had just waited until Hamilton had arrived to see where he was going to be working, then made myself available for that particular task. No doubt there were Daisy Duke and wife beater–clad women on the car wash team, bending over to fill buckets, scrub tires, wring out rags, and spray water on each other. They looked like they were having hot fun in the summertime while they worked, while I looked like somebody's greasy momma tryin'a unpack after a move.

I hadn't quite figured out exactly how I was going to knock this table over inconspicuously to get Hamilton's attention, but when I saw him playfully chasing this female with super-bouncy titties around the parking lot after she sprayed him with water, it was game on. I wasn't just gonna sit back and let her take all of my new man's attention.

Quickly, I made my move to retrieve another box of goods, not too big but not too small. I carried it over to my "noisy" table, pretended to try to sit it down, but intentionally rammed the table with it, and successfully toppled the table over. Oh, I got Hamilton's attention, all right! What I wasn't counting on was that I would actually lose my footing and tumble over the table, still holding on to the box for dear life, my ass landing inside a wok while I was clunked in the head with the top half of a double broiler. Like I'd intended, I drew plenty of attention to myself. Except, now I was deathly embarrassed, sitting on the grass in a sea of cookware. I had one flip-flop on and the other waiting to be located. My sunglasses were tilted on my face, and I had gotten an instant headache

"Oh, Lawd, oh, Lawd, ha' mercy!" I heard an older female hollering while I tried to scramble to my feet. I did see Hamilton and a few other men rushing over, and while a couple of them set the table upright again, Hamilton reached for my hand to help me up off the ground.

"You all right, sista?" he asked, trying to hold back a laugh while he helped me up.

"I think so," I answered, my voice trembling and my knees wobbling. Nothing was hurt but my pride, but when I tried to stand, I came up with the idea to fake an ankle injury and cry out in pain and fall against Hamilton.

"I got you. I got you," he said, reacting with precision and supporting my weight with his strong arms and chest.

Good God almighty, that man felt good against my body! *Thank you, Jesus!* I thought. *You hooked a sista up!*

"Are you okay? What hurts?" he asked, quickly scanning down my body.

"My ankle," I moaned with a fake grimace. "Owww! I'm so sorry."

"No, no, don't apologize. Let's get you a chair. Do we have some ice anywhere?" He motioned to another brother with a head nod to go over to one of the food stations to retrieve some ice.

I'd never faked an injury before, but I had to give it to myself. I was pretty good at it. I put an arm around Hamilton's shoulders, preparing to hop to the nearest chair, and I almost melted when he circled an arm around my waist and easily swept me up into his arms. Why couldn't the chair be way across the churchyard? After taking a few steps, Hamilton eased me to the ground and helped me get settled on the chair.

"Thank you so much. Umm . . . what's your name again?"

"Hamm."

"Thank you so much, Hamm. I'm Candis, by the way." Instead of trying to shake his hand, like we'd done at our first meeting, I grabbed for my ankle to continue my charade.

"Well, Ms. Candis, I hope you're okay." He stooped down at my feet and lifted my foot into his hand. "Let me take a look at it," he said, tilting his head as he inspected my ankle and rubbing it slightly.

"Ssssss," I said with an inhale, and not because it hurt, but because his hands felt so damn good on my skin.

"Hurts, huh?"

"Whew!" I said, instead of straight-out lying.

"Girl, what happened to you?" Dina asked, coming up from wherever she'd been.

"I think I sprained my ankle."

"Doing what?" she asked.

"I don't even know how it happened." Now, that part was true. How in the world did I trip over my own two feet and practically flip over a table?

"By the time Hamm finishes putting his sports therapy on you, I'm sure you will be okay," Dina assured me.

"You're a physical therapist?" I asked, grinning inside.

"Yeah. I work with the Cardinals," he answered, referencing Arizona's National Football League team.

Oh yeah! This dude was just what I was looking for. He was handsome, he had money, he had a solid career, and he didn't mind nurturing a woman. Suddenly, my tumble over the table was worth every bit of embarrassment.

He took a plastic bag of ice and placed it over my uninjured ankle. "Here. Hold this. Let me go get an ACE bandage so we can get it wrapped up. It doesn't look like it's broken."

"Okay," I said, complying. "Thank you, Hamm."

"No problem. I'll be right back," he said, standing to walk to his car.

"I can't take you nowhere." Dina shook her head.

"I know, girl. You got me out here rolling all over the grass, looking a hot mess."

"So what happened?"

"Some kind of way, I fell over a table."

"You fell over a table?" she repeated, then burst into laughter. "I wish I could have seen that!"

"You didn't miss anything." While we chatted, I watched the bouncy-titty girl follow Hamm to his car, stand there for a few minutes, then go back to her post. I was going to have to find out if that was his girlfriend.

Chapter 5

Candis

Hamilton and I had been talking almost daily ever since my fake injury. He'd even dropped by the house a couple of times to check on me and my ankle. I grinned like a man in a strip club whenever I saw his number light up the face of my cell phone, and this time was no different.

"How's that ankle of yours?" he asked.

"I'm much better, thanks to you," I answered. "Thank you again so much."

"It's no problem. It's what I do."

"So you work with the Cardinals, huh? I bet you've seen all kinds of injuries."

"Yeah, I have. Those guys take some really nasty hits out there on the field and do some serious damage to their bodies almost every game."

"I can tell," I replied. "Football is no joke."

"So what do you do for a living?" he asked.

"I'm a professional photographer."

"Sweet. Where do you work?"

"I have my own studio." It felt so good to say that. Made me seem impressive, I thought.

"That's great! Have you ever thought about doing sports photography?"

"Not really."

"You should come out sometime to a practice or something and catch some action shots and see how you like it."

Was he asking me out on a date? That was what it sounded like to me in a roundabout way. And if he was asking, I definitely was going to take him up on it.

"The Cardinals let just anybody into their practices?" I needed him to be more forward with his asking, just in case I was reading him wrong.

"Not exactly, but I know a person that can get you in if you're interested."

"Hmm . . . What does this person look like?" I teased.

"He's, ummm, kinda handsome, a little over six feet, got a few muscles, you know."

"Really?"

"Yeah. Matter fact, I think you might have met him a while back, when you fell on top of some pots and stuff," he said, laughing.

"Oh, gosh! You mean some handsome man other than you saw that too?" I complemented on the sly.

"Naw, just me, just me."

"That was just so mortifying."

"We all have our moments," he said and chuckled.

"Anyway! Can you tell the handsome guy you know that I'd love to go with him to one of those practices?"

"I should be talking to him later on today. I'll see what I can get worked out."

"Sounds great," I said with a smile. "Maybe he and I can get together before the week is out."

"Oh yeah, he will definitely have time this week."

"Cool!"

"All right, well, I'm going to get back out here on this field. . . ."

"And I'm going to get back to editing my photos," I threw in, suddenly realizing that I'd lost control of the call and he was trying to end the call with me, instead of the other way around. "My plate is so full."

"Okay, well, I will call you back this afternoon with a time for later this week."

"If you don't mind, Hamm, can you text me? I have a shoot later on, and I won't be able to answer."

"Oh, okay."

After ending the call, I did a little dance around my studio, excited about the possibilities of dating a new man. A new handsome man who had something going for himself. Yeah. I was liking this church thing. It was working out all right.

As promised, Hamm texted me later that afternoon, offering to pick me up on Thursday, at one o'clock, to take me to the University of Phoenix Stadium for a working date. Although I read the text right away, I didn't confirm until three hours later, then asked if we could make it two o'clock instead, so I wouldn't seem completely available.

Thursday seemed to take forever to come around, but when it came, I was ready. I dressed in a pair of tight capri sports pants that rose to only hip level and a stretchy tank that bared my midriff. I pulled on my Nikes, pulled my hair back like I was going jogging, and loaded my camera bag with a few necessary tools to play around and capture some great shots . . . not of the team, but of Hamm.

It was only a few minutes after two when I saw his car pull up in the lot. Then my cell rang, displaying his number.

"Hey, Candis," he said. "I'm outside in the parking lot. You ready?"

"Yep, I'm on my way," I answered, a bit disappointed that he hadn't gotten out of his car and walked to the door. "Don't make it too serious, Candis," I whispered to myself. "Start as friends. It's all good."

I bounded down the stairs to his car, walked up to the door, and got inside.

"The way you came flying down those stairs, I guess that ankle is really all healed up," he said, glancing down at my feet.

I'd forgotten just that quickly that I was supposed to be getting over an injury. "Yeah, it's been feeling pretty good for the past few days."

"Good. Glad to hear it. Have you eaten yet?"

"Not lunch. I had a bagel a few hours ago for breakfast."

"Well, you need to keep your body fed," he said, glancing down at my abs. "Let's grab something before we get out there to the field."

With my agreement, we stopped at Chipotle Mexican Grill to grab a couple of burritos, then headed out to Glendale. Hamm took me through the employee gate and gave me a tour of the locker room before we went out to where the players were.

"You sure they won't mind me taking photos?"

"Nah. You're with me. It's cool."

I'd never seen so many hard-bodied men so up close and in my reach in my life. Their bodies glistened with sweat, and muscles popped out everywhere on several of them, while a few of them had some rolls that folded over the top of their pants. As taken as I was with Hamm, I found myself lost in a wonderland of flesh and had a great time capturing the players catching and throwing the ball and running up and down the field. Hamm even took me up close and personal, and I got to meet a few of the players and actually shake their hands. I kept my wits about me and didn't act a complete fool, but I was a little starstruck.

"Let me get a few shots of you, Hamm," I requested as together we walked toward the stands.

"You want pictures of little old me? Shucks, I ain't nobody."

"If it weren't for you, I might be walking with a limp right now," I said and laughed, still living out my lie from community day.

"I'm sure you know how to get yourself medical attention when it's necessary. You would have been just fine had I not been around."

"Maybe so, but not without an exorbitant medical bill to go with it," I replied, pointing the camera at him. "And I definitely wouldn't have been swept off my feet and have found myself resting comfortably in the doctor's arms."

"Oh, you liked that, huh?" He smiled and came toward me with his arms ready to lift me. I practically jumped in his arms this time, except instead of assuming a cradle position, I wrapped my legs at his waist. "Whoa!" he exclaimed, grabbing my thighs and holding me up.

"What? Am I too heavy?"

"Not at all," he whispered in a tone that suggested he was perfectly fine with my weight and positioning.

"How long do you think you could hold me like this?" I winked.

Backing me into a wall and pushing his hips forward, he answered, "We can find out. I'm pretty strong, you know." With a quick shift, he raised me up into his arms, bringing my pelvis up to his chest, and then proposed lifting me even higher than that.

"Okay, okay, let me down," I ordered and giggled. "Let me down."

"Oh, don't get scared now." He seductively bit his bottom lip and glanced at my breasts, which were just a quick jerk away from his face.

"Being scared is not what I'm scared of."

"What is it, then?" he asked, still threatening to toss me up around his neck so that my crotch would meet his face.

"I don't want your girlfriend to catch us. She might not appreciate me too much."

"If I had one, you'd have something to worry about."

"So you're not seeing anyone?" I asked, not wanting to make assumptions about his answer.

"Not at all," he said, looking up at me. "How do I know your boyfriend is not going to come popping up from around the corner, wondering what you're doing up in my arms?"

"If I had one, you'd have something to worry about," I answered with a wink.

"In that case, I think I could hold you like this all night, every night."

But just a few nights and a few dinners later, that "all night, every night" became a thing of the past--and so did Hamm. Regardless of my calls and texts, it was like Hamm and I had never even met. Even when I went to church after that, Hamm avoided me like an STD. Couldn't get him to call me back if my quasi-sprained ankle depended on it. I was more embarrassed now than I had been when I'd fallen. I'd quickly and easily given myself away, thinking that somebody like Hamm, a churchgoing, worshipping man, would have more respect for me, or for the situation, than to just completely dis me. That was what those no-good busters in the street did, but I didn't expect that from a church guy.

I'd played myself, but lesson learned. Church or no church, all men were after only one thing, and after they got it, they were gone.

"What do you mean, this time?" I couldn't help myself.

"You know how Russell is. The same way he was with you. Noncommittal. This is, like, her third time setting a date, but she's talking like it's really gonna happen on this go-round."

"Are you going?" I asked, still not making eye contact.

"I haven't decided. I might."

"Oh." I had mixed feelings about Dina's indecision. I wanted her to say, "Hell no, I ain't going to that wench's shower." She knew my history with Russell, but maybe she didn't know that sometimes I still thought about him . . . a lot. Never to the point that I'd picked up the phone in the past year and called him, but I would often wish I could. In my imagination he'd answer the phone and say, "Baby, I was just thinking about you, wishing I could hear your voice. Wondering how I could make it right between us." But that would be a lie. Russell never did put too much effort into us being a couple. It just wasn't what he wanted. I would have liked for things to have turned out differently. I'd wanted the whole marriage, two kids, a house, and a dog thing with him. Regardless of the many ways I tried to make myself "the one," simply put, I just wasn't the woman for him.

"Y'all want some more wine?" I stood and started toward the refrigerator to hide my face for a moment. The coolness from the fridge helped to keep my tears at bay, and I needed all the help I could get right now. I didn't want to cry over Russell, and I really didn't want Dina and Celeste to see it.

To be fair to Latrice, she wasn't really a wench. From what I knew of her, she was a nice girl, one of Dina's hair clients. I just couldn't believe he was marrying her

Chapter 6

Candis

"Candis, I heard that Russell is getting married."
Russell? What? Hearing Dina say those words felt like a blow to my head with a baseball bat, but I didn't want it to show. "Really? Good for him."
"Guess who he's marrying," she continued.
I shrugged my shoulders, pretending to be preoccupied with engagement photos I shot of her and Bertrand that were spread out on my kitchen table. "It doesn't matter to me," I lied.
"Well, I'm going to tell you, anyway. Girl, he is marrying Latrice Chambers."
"That's nice," I replied without hesitation, instead of verbalizing my true thoughts.
Latrice Chambers? Four-kids-having Latrice? Big belly, bigger booty Latrice? Twenty- eight-pounds-of-weave- and cat-claw-nails-wearing Latrice? Humph!
"Look at this one. It's so cute." I pushed a photo across the table toward her and Celeste while I tried to digest what Dina had just said. First of all, I wasn't sure if she was being a friend or a foe by telling me that news. Why would she want to share that with me? But, on the other hand, I was sure to hear it eventually, and I guess it didn't matter whom I'd heard it from.
"I think it's serious this time, because I got an invitation to her bridal shower," Dina added.

instead of marrying me. What about me wasn't good enough for him?

"I'll have a little bit more," Celeste said, picking up her glass to sip the last little bit from it before she handed it to me.

"None for me. Thanks," Dina answered. She never drank, so really the offer was solely for Celeste.

Russell and I did what I called "dating" for about eighteen months. He called it 'just hanging out." I was such a dummy for choosing to believe he felt more in his heart for me than what his mouth was willing to say, instead of believing the truth that there was really nothing between us as far as he was concerned. Well, initially, I could understand there being nothing. We were just getting to know each other, and not everybody falls in love, or even strong like, at first sight, but I sure did.

Everything about the man appealed to me, from his piercing gray eyes and gleaming smile to the way he was dressed in tailor-made suits, to his slightly over six-foot build, to him owning his own insurance company. I was tired of dating blue-collar workers who often smelled like sweat, grease, and dirt. Not that there was anything wrong with blue-collar professions, but it was just something about a professional man in a suit that made my goody box hungry.

We'd met at a Phoenix Chamber of Commerce event and started seeing each other on the sly, under the guise of business meetings. The first few meetings, we talked heavily about my "insurance needs" and made some small talk about our personal lives. He was single with a set of preteen daughters, had never been married but had a peaceable relationship with his girls' mother, and had owned his own insurance agency for almost ten years.

I thought we'd hit it off pretty well, enjoying each other's conversation, sharing business strategies, and bouncing things off of each other, and I tried not to be too transparent with my personal interest in him, although he did a little flirting. I'd tricked myself into believing that men didn't flirt with women they weren't interested in. We started calling each other every day, meeting for lunch, watching movies at each other's homes, all cuddled up on the couch, eating out of the same popcorn bowl. And eventually we started having sex. And once I started taking my panties off on a regular basis, in my book, he was my boyfriend. In his book, I was just a friend who afforded him a lot of benefits. How was a man spending the night at my house four and five nights out of the week, getting all the sex he could handle—including the extras—while I washed his clothes, cooked him meals, and even babysat his kids on the weekends when he had visitation but had to work, not considered a relationship? I didn't understand what was so "just friends" about that. I was playing the part of the wife, to say the least, thinking and hoping that one day he'd claim me as his very own, to have and to hold, etcetera.

I was cool with that for a little while, knowing that having sex didn't exactly make a relationship, but after several months of cooking him dinner, helping him with some of his business tasks, and freaking him like I was getting paid for it, I expected an official title. Like a fool, I thought he would eventually come around, but all I was doing was giving him 100 percent free punanny. I never got a thing for it, but not so satisfying sex and hurt feelings. Even though he wasn't even all that great in the bedroom, I was willing to settle. I mean, it wasn't *that* bad. Not really. Hell, who was I kidding? It was awful. He never really took the time to make love to me gently and tenderly, like I wanted at least every now and then, but he was always in a rush to satisfy his own selfish needs. Thrusting in and out of me like a wild dog, rarely lasting more than ten minutes, then rushing home or to work or just to sleep. But at least he wasn't married.

Clearly he just wasn't that into me, but because I was in love with him, I just couldn't let him go. It's stupid, I know, but that was my reality. I just kept trying to win him. Kept cooking, kept trying to add value to his life, kept letting him in the temple, and kept believing that although he wouldn't say it with his mouth, I was his girlfriend and he was in love with me too. He even took me to Jamaica one time for a whole week.

We lay out on those beaches, wrapped in each other's arms, watching the sun rise and set, kissed lover's kisses and, of course, had sex like we were on our honeymoon. When our plane touched the ground back in Phoenix, I was all souped up in the head, thinking that finally we had something defined, but then I opened my mouth and asked, "Baby, what do you call this that we are doing? I mean, where do things stand with us?"

"What do you mean, Candis? We just came from a beautiful trip to paradise, and you have questions about where we stand?" Question avoidance. That was typical for him.

"Yes, because I need to know. I need to hear it out of your mouth." Mentally, I crossed my fingers, hoping he'd say what I wanted to hear.

"Well, you know," he began with a shrug. "We're real good friends."

My heart sank like a stone. One thing I'd learned for sure was if you didn't know where your relationship stood, you knew exactly where it stood.

I was silent as he drove me home, then helped me bring my luggage in the house. Then I kissed his cheek and said, "Thanks for a great trip."

"You're welcome, baby." He grinned like he was proud of himself for presumably making me really happy. "You deserved it."

Guess that was my booby prize.

After we said our good-byes that day, I stopped calling him and taking his calls. It took about three days of ignoring his calls for him to show up at my house unannounced, asking me what the hell was going on.

"Nothing. I've just been busy," I answered. "I just don't have time for my friends like I used to, I guess. I've had to refocus on other things."

"Candis, don't ignore me like this. You know you and I make a good team."

Interpretation: He was getting his cake and ice cream and eating them too, then licking the bowl and going back for seconds and thirds, and he wasn't ready to let it go. Really, who would turn down free cake and ice cream?

"Yeah, I know. I've just been busy."

"I think you're trying to run from me."

"Hmm," I commented with a shrug.

He stayed for another thirty minutes, trying to get me to embrace, kiss, and no doubt have sex with him, but I wouldn't crack. I was done spinning my wheels in the mud of our "relationship."

"Well, call me when you get a chance, babe." Russell pecked my cheek and headed toward the door. "I look forward to seeing you later."

I didn't call him again until three months later, and only because I needed a physical tune-up. You know, a little maintenance work. It was a mistake, because all it did was reengage my emotions and get me hoping for a serious relationship all over again. When I realized all I was getting was more of the same, I weaned myself off of him for good. I was spent. I was done. I'd given him all I had, and I had to come to terms with the fact that he just didn't want me. Then here it was, not even a good six months later, and his ass was getting married to Latrice Chambers? He better be glad that I'd given up keying cars and busting windows in my early twenties.

Although I refused to speak to or see Russell following that trip to Jamaica, I did spend a fair amount of time scoping his Facebook profile, doing what was called Facebook drive-bys. I just couldn't help myself initially. I'd mosey around to see what he was posting, if there were new photos, who was in them, who was liking and commenting on his stuff. There were a few females who'd posted on his wall, but nothing that looked interesting. Why I cared, I didn't know. Well, yes, I did. It was because he still consumed a lot of space in my mind. I missed him. I missed the good times we'd shared, the laughter, the fun moments. I thought we made a great couple, but he constantly denied me the title of girlfriend. I wondered what would happen if I texted him. Would he answer me back? Or suppose I left a comment? I was feening for the man bad. Not because I wanted more of a dried-up relationship. I just missed him. After a few months of privately stalking him, I eventually stopped. He wasn't a very public person, anyway, and hardly ever had anything new posted to his wall. But now, with this new marriage announcement, my curiosity was renewed.

After looking through Dina and Bertrand's engagement photos and chatting some more, Dina and Celeste decided to head home, and I was on my own for the rest of the evening. I was supposed to be online, completing some marketing tasks for my photo studio, but I kept getting distracted by people's constant Facebook status updates. As I clicked around from one profile to the next, I found myself on Russell's profile, just to be nosy. My heart dropped when I saw engagement pictures of him and his so-called fiancée wearing big smiles and sharing loving embraces, being the happy couple he and I were supposed to be. I felt my old disappointment slowly creeping up inside me, with anger closely following. He rejected me for that? For her? He deserved a good in-box cussin' out.

"Let me stop before I do something stupid," I told myself, reshifting my interest to my news feed. There I saw an interesting post from one of my acquaintances.

Question: Is love enough? Simple question, right? I wonder if most people believe that love conquers all, and that as long as two people love each other, they should be together, and no matter the problem, they can/should work it out simply because they love each other. So is love enough? What do you think?

I wanted to post, "Hell to the no!" I thought about how much emotion I had wasted on Russell and how he hadn't paid me a bit of attention—not real attention. And as much as I loved him, it was not enough to build a relationship, nor was it enough to make me want to stick around and hope that one day he'd develop deeper feelings for me. Just as I set my fingers on the keyboard to offer up my opinion, another person posted. His answer caught my attention and intrigued me.

SeanMichael Monroe
Yes. Love is patient; love is kind; love is not selfish or easily provoked, etc. I think love predicated on the premise of what true love is—not an emotion or gushy feelings—yes, it's enough. Few

people know how to love like that or have experienced that kind of love.

Before I left my comment, I clicked on LIKE for Sean-Michael's comment, then clicked his name. His profile was public, so I perused his photos first, eyeing shots of a nicely tanned brother with a wide smile and bright eyes. His face reminded me of Brian McKnight. By the time I looked through all fifty-seven of his posted pictures, he'd left another comment on the thread.

SeanMichael Monroe
Love conquers all, but finding it can seem like finding a pot of gold at the end of a rainbow.

Candis I'mTheOne Turner
Have you ever found gold, SeanMichael?

SeanMichael Monroe
Found it? I don't think so. Not in a person. Given it? Plenty of times. It wasn't reciprocated.

Candis I'mTheOne Turner
I know that feeling. It sucks. I still say no.

SeanMichael Monroe
I think if you say no, it only means you have yet to experience true love and have a warped perception of what love is.

Other people started adding to the thread, making it more challenging for me to respond directly to Sean-Michael's comments, so I went back to his wall, clicked on MESSAGE, and in-boxed him.

Hi SeanMichael,

It was getting a little crowded on the wall, so I hope you don't mind me shooting you an in-box message. I like your perception, and I think you're right. Some people just don't realize what love is, or what it means. I'd be interested in knowing what it means to you.

Hello Ms. Candis,

Like I said in my initial comment, based off of what is found in the Bible, love is a lot of things that we don't even consider when we call ourselves being in love or looking for love. Love is patient; love is kind; love doesn't envy or boast and isn't prideful. Love does not dishonor people, and love is not selfish or easily angered. Love keeps no record of wrongs and does not enjoy evil. Love is happy about the truth; it protects, trusts, hopes and perseveres; and love never fails.

I believe the way we generally measure love is through how we feel in our emotions. We look for butterflies, rainbows, and chocolate candy. We measure love by giddiness and mushiness, and it can't be measured in those terms and be called love. Those are called feelings, and feelings change from day to day. Sometimes you feel like going to work, and sometimes you don't, so you can't just be guided by your feelings.

I was impressed with SeanMichael's response, and we carried on with our in-box messages for the rest of the evening. He shared with me how he'd been in love with a young lady who was very materialistic and measured love by what he could or could not give her. They'd had a baby together, but the mother was on drugs, unbeknownst to him, and it led to the baby's early birth and unfortunate demise. In one of his messages to me he said, "See, that wasn't love, because what she did was selfish. She didn't consider my feelings or our baby's health when she was out in the street, doing crack. Love is not selfish." His insights got me to thinking about what I was looking for from Russell and whether I loved him. I felt like I did. I sure as hell was patient and kind.

I also found out that SeanMichael was thirty-two, single, went to church every Sunday, worked for Exxon, and loved music. It was too bad he lived all the way on the other side of the United States of America. If he didn't, I would have been trying to meet up with him. There were a lot of miles between Phoenix, Arizona, and Baltimore, Maryland. Oh well, online friendships were always good.

The next day, when I logged into my Facebook account, there was a message from SeanMichael in my in-box.

Good morning!
I enjoyed our conversation last night. May your day be filled with true love.
SeanMichael

After that, SeanMichael and I communicated every day in some form or fashion. After a series of in-box messages, we exchanged phone numbers, and I became accustomed to hearing from him every morning, at the start of my day. I found his energy refreshing and loved that he was too far from me for our friendship to be anything other than platonic.

Chapter 7

Dina

"I don't know about Bertrand," I'd said to Celeste and Candis during one of our lunch outings several months ago, when he'd first proposed.

"Why? What's wrong with him?" Candis had asked.

"That's the thing. Nothing is wrong with him. He's, like, the perfect guy." I shrugged.

"So what's your problem?" Candis stretched her eyes at me. "He's not abusive, he's not a womanizer, he works, and he's straight."

"And he got money," Celeste threw in.

Even with all the great things Bertrand brought to the table, I just didn't feel that thing a woman's heart felt when she really loved someone. And I didn't know why I didn't feel it. On paper, he was everything I wanted in a man. And he wanted to marry me. How could I say no to a man who always treated me the way I wanted a man to treat me, who had his life together, and who was handsome to boot? I couldn't think of a single reason on God's green and blue earth why I should reject him. Except I didn't love him, and I was mad at myself about that. I wanted to love him because he was so good to me. I'd tried to make myself love him, but I couldn't just magically create what wasn't there.

He didn't make my heart go pitter-patter or give me butterflies. Nonetheless, I was convinced that with some time, I would grow to really love him. Like people who were set up in arranged marriages had to do. Didn't they eventually fall in love with each other? Maybe after a baby or something? I was certain that once we were married and he became the center of my day—the same spot I'd given to my dog of an ex-husband, Cameron—the butterflies and the pitter-patters would come.

"I know all that, but . . . I don't know. Maybe he is just too perfect." It was the best thing I could come up with.

"What the hell do you mean?" Celeste asked, wrinkling up her nose like the garbage truck had just emptied a load of foul rubbish in the room. "I've never heard of somebody not wanting to be with someone because he's too perfect. That just sounds crazy."

"I can't exactly put my finger on it," I lied.

"Well, I don't know what you're trippin' about. Look at that great big Kobe Bryant–sized ring on your finger," Candis added, grabbing my hand, glancing at the ring, then slinging my hand away just as quickly. "Girl, you would be a fool not to marry that man."

At that point, I decided to shut up about it. They were making me feel silly for not being more excited about marrying Bertrand, but the fact was, I just didn't love him.

So why did I accept his proposal in the first place? Well, I'd never admit this to Celeste or Candis, because it sounded so fickle and callous, but security was one of the main reasons. That and sex, which was consistently mind blowing. Yep. It was.

Bertrand could put it down in the bedroom, but I was spiritually uncomfortable with having sex outside of marriage. Bertrand didn't share my moral convictions, but every time we did it, which was a lot, I was scared that I was going to run into some impending doom as punishment for sleeping with a man who wasn't my husband. And whispering a silent prayer of repentance after every session made me feel like I was taking God's mercy, grace, and forgiveness for granted. It was hard trying to enjoy sex with your man when you thought Jesus might crack the sky at any moment and send you straight to hell.

I felt like such a hypocrite on Sunday mornings, trying to raise my hands for worship, knowing that I'd just gotten out of Bertrand's bed or he'd just gotten out of mine. The Bible said it was better to marry than to burn, so I decided to marry, because for as long as we'd been sexually involved, I just couldn't see myself suddenly cutting that part of our relationship off. Bertrand wouldn't get it; he would probably think I was giving the goodies to someone else if I stopped giving them to him, so I *had* to get married.

I liked Bertrand alot. He was kind, warm, sensitive, and he treated me well. He had a good job working for the state of Arizona, in the zoning department, which he'd been in for ten years. He didn't have a criminal record, and there were no baby mamas lurking in the wings, although he did have an ex-wife, but they had long ago gone their separate ways. Bertrand was honest, loved his parents, owned a home, wasn't on drugs, and wasn't gay, not that I knew about, anyway. And then add to that, he had money in the bank and was all into financial investments, portfolios, and planning for retirement. I, on the other hand, was trying to come up with a plan to keep my bills paid for another month. Business at the shop had been slow. People weren't getting their hair done as often as they used to, which really rocked my budget and made my money super tight. I wasn't looking for a financial savior, but I knew

Bertrand could take care of me. For once in my life I wouldn't have to live paycheck to paycheck.

Bertrand and I lived separately, in our own homes. Shacking up definitely wasn't my style, pending nuptials or not. I had my house; he had his. I had my bills; he had his. I had my money. . . . Well, actually, I had none, but he had his. I did, by the grace of God, manage to keep a roof over my head, but almost every bill I had was delinquent. My phone rang constantly, with people looking for me and wanting their money. When I compared my financial situation to Bertrand's, along with taking into consideration the fact that he treated me so well and seemed to have his life together, I knew marrying him was a no-brainer. He was a good man and what woman doesn't want that? I knew too many females who fell in love first and still weren't in the best of relationships, so really. . . love wasn't all that important. It could come later.

Bertrand had no idea about me being so behind on my bills, because I had too much pride to tell him. I didn't want him thinking I expected him to pay my bills, even though we were engaged. Sometimes he made me feel like he just wanted to be engaged and nothing more, because every time I'd proposed a wedding date, he'd come up with a reason why the date wouldn't work. January was his birthday month, and he didn't want to share it with a wedding anniversary. February, Valentine's Day. March, his mom's birthday. Before he could tell me he didn't want our anniversary competing with April Fools' Day, I cut him off.

"Bertrand, there's something going on every month of every year. That's really not a reason not to set a date." I was a tiny bit anxious to stop living a sinful lifestyle and stop struggling with bills. And I did feel *something* for Bertrand. I just wasn't sure it was love, but in the words of Tina Turner, "What's love got to do, got to do with it?"

"Well, let me think about it," he'd said. He always said that when he wanted to avoid making a decision or giving an answer.

It was such an awful feeling, trying to push someone into actually marrying me. I mean, he did propose, so did he want to marry me or not? Instead of letting myself get frustrated, I figured I'd let things fall into place at a natural and unforced pace. I just didn't foresee it taking this long. I thought he would have married me (and financially rescued me) by now. Guess I had to wait it out.

Other than that, Bertrand was a sweetheart. He spoiled me ridiculously; there was nothing that I wanted that he wouldn't give me. The strange thing was, it seemed to apply only to material things, not financial things, and that made me confused. I liked blingy gifts as much as the next woman, but last month, when my cell phone got cut off for nonpayment, I would have rather he'd paid the bill for me than given me that sparkly Pandora-style charm bracelet. And groceries would have been nice over dinners out. Hell, I could cook. I didn't complain about it, because I didn't want to seem ungrateful, but he had to know that I needed help with bills. He had to know that I was strapped for cash, since my phone was off. How else would I be, given that I had a dwindling clientele and had time to meet him for lunch almost every day? It just didn't make sense to me when he didn't offer to get my phone put back on. It was like he really didn't want to help.

Just last week he was at my house and overheard me on the phone with a bill collector. Granted he could hear only my half of the conversation, but it didn't take a rocket scientist to figure out what was going on when I was saying stuff like, "I'm sorry. I just don't have the money to make the payment right now. I'm not sure, but I will try to bring it current as soon as I can." I hadn't wanted to take the call in front of him, but then I thought it would be a good way for him to see indirectly that I was struggling financially, without having to actually tell him . . . or ask for money. I hung up the phone and let out a sigh.

"Who was that?" he asked.

I shook my head with a sigh. "Bill collector."

"Oh."

That was his answer. "Oh." There was no probing to find out which bill it was, how much money I needed, nothing like that. Just "oh." Maybe I should have gotten off the phone, looked directly at him, and asked for a thousand dollars. That was just too close to begging to me, and as my fiancé, I expected him to be more attentive and naturally responsive to my needs. They say the squeaky wheel gets the oil and closed mouths don't get fed, but if you saw the wheel was on the verge of falling off the damn wagon, did it really need to start squeaking? Maybe I just expected too much. After all, it was my financial mess, not his. I just couldn't believe he'd sit back and watch me flounder, though. Especially when he was telling me he loved me all the time. But love doesn't pay the bills, though, huh?

The other thing about Bertrand was, he was super clingy and expected me to spend every moment of my day with him. If for some reason I couldn't do that, he needed an hourly update on where I was and what I was doing, and he had to know if I was okay. He wanted me to call him when I left the house in the morning for work; once I arrived at my job, to let him know I'd gotten there safely; at least three times during

my workday, so that he would know that I was thinking of him; and then once more when I left work and
was on my way home. It was sweet at first just knowing
that someone cared about me enough to want to hear
from me all the time, but after a while, that mess got
old. That was way too much calling in my day. Don't let
me mess around and be too busy to answer my phone.
He'd have an attitude for at least a day.

After spinning my last client out of the door, I dialed
Bertrand's number as I tidied up my workstation for
the day.

"Hey, babe. I'm running a little bit late. I'll be home
in about thirty minutes, so give me about forty-five or
so." He was picking me up for a dinner and movie date.

Once I got home, I rushed in the house, took a quick
shower, and stepped into a silk asymmetrical handker-
chief halter dress that he'd bought me. I'd worn it only
once before, and it got me compliments from everyone
I came across that day. I stepped into a pair of smoky
blue stilettos just as Bertrand tapped on the door.

As he soaked in my appearance, his eyes and his
smile confirmed how amazing I looked, and then his
commentary added to it.

"Look at you looking like a million bucks." He nodded. "I like that, baby. You look good!"

"Thanks. It's just a little something from the back of
my closet that my man picked for me," I teased.

"Your man has good taste. What else you got in your
closet?" he asked, thinking about the night before.

The hanging rack in my closet had somehow pulled
away from the wall, dumping all my clothes on the
floor. Bertrand had made an assessment, had gone
home to get a few tools, had come back, and then re-

paired it for me. As he helped me move my clothes from my bed, where I'd placed them temporarily while he fixed the rack, our bodies kept brushing, until it turned into a game of fondling.

Standing behind me, he slid a single hand beneath my T-shirt, tracing a path up my back. With almost no effort he unhooked my bra, then circled both his hands around to my breasts while he planted kisses on my neck. His throbbing manhood pressed against my behind as he let out a slow moan. I turned in his arms, and our lips collided in lustful passion. While he groped my body, I groped the wall for the light switch, then reached for and closed the door, immersing us in complete darkness. In minutes, we stripped each other of clothes and caressed each other's flesh.

"Look how you have me," he said, taking one of my hands and giving me his hardness.

I massaged him for a few minutes, and there, in the darkness, I took him in my mouth. Bertrand gasped for breath and held it for a few seconds while I slowly worked my tongue along his length.

"Ahhhhh," he moaned, encouraging me to continue. "Baby, yes!" he cried out, gently placing his hands in my hair, then pumping his hips slightly forward, show- ing me what he wanted. I loved to hear him express his pleasure, and I met his request, becoming more aggressive with my movements and listening to his moans grow louder.

After a few minutes, he pulled away and dropped to the floor, guiding me to lie back. He trailed kisses from my neck to the center of my Tootsie Pop, then worked some tongue magic on me that was out of this world. When Bertrand finished with me, I barely knew my own name. Knowing that he'd satisfied me, he eased his way back on top of me and pushed his stiffness into my moistness, and together, in a series of heated breaths, pants, and chants, we took each other to ecstasy. Then we lay there on the floor, caressing each other, trying to recoup.

"Why don't you just come on and move in with me?" Bertrand whispered, sucking on my breasts.

"Because we're not married yet, babe. I'm not exactly comfortable with that."

"So what are you going to do about your bills? You just can't let them keep getting behind," he said, drawing circles on my arm with his finger.

"I don't know." I shrugged. "I'm trying to get a second job."

"You don't have to do that," he answered. "You're going to be my wife, and a real man takes care of what's his. If anything, I'll get a second job."

Now, I wasn't all into a man paying my bills—I liked to stand on my own two feet—but hearing that he would take pride in taking care of me was like music to my ears. He was trying to provide for me, and I'd learned that that was one of the ways to tell if a man was really serious about the woman he was seeing. It was one of the three Ps. Profess his love, provide, and protect. Bertrand had already professed his love for me, and it was apparent.

I pulled him more closely to me and massaged his head.

"I got you, baby," he whispered.

It made me smile. My pride wasn't comfortable with him bailing me out, but my wallet sure was. It felt good knowing that Bertrand had my back. Moving in early wouldn't be so bad, would it? Engaged couples lived together all the time on their way to the altar. As long as we were at least planning the wedding, I guess I could be all right with moving in a little bit early. Moving in would mean no rent expense, no power or water bill to pay, no extra Internet bill, and all that other stuff. Bertrand would pay them since this was his house, and he was used to paying them, anyway. It would relieve me of paying at least a thousand dollars a month, and that could come in right handy for wedding planning or paying off my credit cards.

There was no sense in paying for two roofs when we needed only one, especially for a broke girl like me.

We finally pulled ourselves up from the floor, re-dressed, and brought my closet back to order, grinning and giggling at each other the whole time. By the time we finished, we decided that I'd move in to his house after giving my apartment complex the required thirty-day notice.

"Now that we've got everything put back, I guess it's time to pull it all down and start packing," I said and laughed.

We started packing that following week and slowly transitioned my things to his place. Before the month was over, the only thing left in my apartment was my bed and a few necessities, but I wanted to stay there as long as I could.

Now with just a week before I had to be out of my apartment, Bertrand hit me with the unexpected.

"I have something to show you," he said with a smile as we rode to dinner.

"What is it?" He was always surprising me with gifts and whatnot, so I grinned, expecting something wonderful.

"I'll let you see it when I stop the car."

"Is it something to wear? Like new boots," I sang.

"Not exactly." Bertrand chuckled, reaching over and rubbing my thigh. "You'll see."

Once he parked the car, he reached in the backseat and retrieved a plastic folder, which he handed to me with a grin.

Unsuspecting, I opened it up and saw the cover page. It read: "Prenuptial Agreement between Bertrand R. Peyton and Dina K. Winston."

Did this man just slap me with a prenup? Caught completely off guard and shocked, I jerked my head toward him.

"What is this?" I waved the folder at him.

"I thought it would be a good idea that we had one before we got married," he said, looking rather smug and proud of himself.

I, on the other hand, was more than offended and was at a loss for words other than "Take me home."

"What? Why? I thought we were going to catch a movie." His grin faded as he darted his eyes between my grimace and the folder.

"Bertrand, take me home please," I stated again, fighting back several emotions that were trying to release themselves from my insides.

"What's wrong?"

"How are you going to give me this on a casual ride in the car?" I asked, my anger begging to bleed through.

"Babe, I'm sorry if I offended you. I just thought—"

"Don't think. Just take me home."

Bertrand pushed out a breath, shifted the car into gear, and in silence drove me back to my front door, where he'd picked me up just minutes before.

"Dina, I really didn't mean—"

"Don't worry about it," I said, brushing it off. "I'm just not feeling well." I tucked the folder under my arm, pushed the car door open, and step out onto the pavement.

"You could at least let me walk you to the door."

"That's okay. I'm fine." I slammed the car door shut before he could say another word.

Once inside, I slumped on the couch, opened the folder, and read over the words. Bertrand had inserted various elements into a template, starting with his house. For the next thirty minutes, I gazed over the papers, and every word that I read made me seethe. In a nutshell, he'd spelled out that everything he owned at the time of our marriage would remain his if we should happen to split. There were about eight pages of legalese concerning his assets and their respective values, and his debt, which was absolutely none, other than his mortgage. There was one more page about him, which showed his net worth at about a half a million dollars. The last two pages were devoted to me and what he knew my assets to be. Since all I had was bills and a little raggedy car, along with a car note, my net worth was far into the red. I was insulted and embarrassed.

I tossed the folder onto the table, rose from the couch, and decided to soak in the tub with a glass of wine to try to get my thoughts together. Once I was seated in the hot water and John Legend was crooning through my iPod to calm my nerves, I tried to think more sensibly. Maybe I was upset because I didn't think about presenting him with a prenup, but I had this silly notion in my head that what was mine would be his, and what was his would become mine, and we would live this nice, long, happy life together, have a couple of children, and thirty or forty years from now sit out on the front porch with glasses of sweet tea, reading the newspaper. But now I had to think differently, and actually a prenup *was* a good idea . . . if I had something to my name other than a ton of debt.

I finished my bath, reclined on the bed, and called Candis.

"What are you doing?" I asked.

"I'm on another call," she said. I could hear the bubbles in her voice.

"With who? You sure sound happy about it."

"Just a guy I met. Nothing big."

"What guy? You let me find out you got a secret boyfriend . . . ," I said, chastising her.

"Girl, it ain't nothing like that. His name is SeanMichael, and we're just talking, that's all."

"Mmm-hmm. That's how it all gets started." She joined me in a light chuckle. "I guess I'll call Celeste, then. I'll talk to you later."

"Okay, girl."

I dialed Celeste's number, but her phone just rang. "Celeste, call me when you get this message. I need to vent."

Chapter 8

Candis

I was glad Dina didn't try to hold me hostage on the phone, although she did sound like something was wrong. I promised myself to follow up with her later as I switched my line back over to SeanMichael.

"I'm back, baby," I said in what was just a hair above a whisper. SeanMichael and I had been talking voice to voice for a good while now and had embraced terms of endearment. I'd never been in a long-distance relationship before, and honestly, I was apprehensive about saying I was in one now, but more and more, it was feeling that way. He had me jumping for my phone every time it vibrated, not wanting to miss his call or text. I'd caught myself grinning when I saw it was him and whatnot. I felt silly because we'd never even met, and here I was, letting my emotions get involved.

"I missed you."

"I wasn't even gone a full minute," I said in a giggly schoolgirl voice. That was exactly how SeanMichael made me feel—like a schoolgirl. Like Fantasia scribbling *X*s and *O*s in a notebook, all dreamy eyed.

"And that was too long," he mumbled. "You know what I'd wish if I had one right now?"

"What's that?"

"I'd wish that I was in your arms or that you were in mine."

"I'd like that," I said in all honesty. I was falling in love with him, but that notion sounded too ridiculous in my thinking for me to allow myself to dwell on it. "So what's holding you back?"

"Holding me back from what?"

"From allowing me to be in your arms." That was my way of asking him to come see me without just putting it out there.

"Money," he blurted out in a guffaw. "I was going to try to come out there, but do you know how much a ticket between here and there is?" His tone was both incredulous and rhetorical.

"I've never been out there, so I have no idea, but let me look. I have my laptop right here." With a quick Google search, I found a few quotes, the least expensive one being just a couple hundred dollars. I shared. "I see a ticket that's only two sixty-five."

"Yeah, I can't afford that," he countered just as soon as my words hit his ear.

"That's not that bad."

"It is if you don't have it," he said and chuckled.

"I can understand you not having it planned in the budget," I said, trying to understand his angle. "But you can save up for it. I'm having a party for my birthday, and I'd love for you to come."

"The way my check gets garnished . . ."

Garnished? What?

"I hardly have enough money to get stuff I need." SeanMichael sounded defeated and relieved at the same time, like he had been waiting to tell me that and had finally gotten it out.

"What do you mean?" It wasn't that I didn't understand what he'd said. I was just taken aback by it. His check was being garnished? *Don't tell me he has ten kids somewhere and is being forced to pay child sup-*

port. This man better not be trying to fix his mouth to ask me to send him some money, I thought. "Why is your check being garnished?"

"I just had some bills that got out of control," he said, trying to dismiss the matter.

But I had more questions. Usually when people didn't pay a regular bill, it just ended up on their credit report, but garnishments were generally for things like taxes, credit cards, student loans, and . . . child support.

"What kind of bills?" I quizzed, taking a risk.

"Just some stuff."

"Stuff like what? Like, umm . . . taking care of some children?" To me, that sounded better than child support.

"Naw," he rushed to say. "I told you I don't have any kids."

"Oh."

I didn't want to push too much, because it really was none of my business. SeanMichael wasn't really my man, and he owed me no explanations. But one thing was for sure. If he was being garnished, he didn't pay his bills on time, and if he didn't pay his bills on time, he was probably broke. I tried to change the subject, but I couldn't help it. I needed to . . . well, wanted to know more, because one thing I didn't need in my life was a broke-ass man.

"So is it, like, credit card debt or something?"

"Girl, do you know how much trouble you can get into with a credit card?" he said, like I'd just named the worse possible debt ever. "I don't use credit cards. I pay for everything in cash."

If his wages were being garnished, he probably couldn't even get a credit card, but I kept that thought to myself. It took me a bit more prying and some strategic questioning, but SeanMichael did spill the beans.

Came to find out he owed on a car loan from a buy-here, pay-here car lot. The car had been repossessed after he tried to hide it for a few months while he was between jobs.

"Until I get that taken care of, I just have to catch the bus or walk to work. The walking keeps me in shape," he said.

I guess that was how he made himself feel better about not having a car. SeanMichael was a nice guy and all, but damn, he had only a little minimum-wage job, a garnished check, and no car. Red flag on the play!

Chapter 9

Dina

"He gave you a what?" Celeste gasped when I told her about the prenup. "Who is he? A descendant of John D. Rockefeller?"

"I guess so, girl. I knew he had a few dollars, but I didn't know I was marrying into real money," I joked, but really, nothing was funny.

"What did you say?"

"I told him to take me home, so he did. I need you to help me think rationally." The prenup did upset me, but now that I was calmer, I could think about it more sensibly. What would I do with my stuff if something happened and the marriage didn't work out? I surely wouldn't want him to have possession of it, just like he didn't want me to have any of his stuff.

"Well, in this day and time, unfortunately, you do have to think about these things, so you can't completely hate on him for being proactive," Celeste observed.

"Yeah, but did he have to just give it to me like that? We could have at least had a discussion about it first or something. He just pulled it out of the backseat and gave it to me like he was handing me a box of chocolates or a birthday card."

"I have to agree that that was pretty tacky, but look beyond that point and look at what was really going on.

He wants to protect his stuff, and you should want to protect yours too."

"But don't you think that sets a negative tone for the marriage?"

"Well, kind of, but at the same time, you can't be too careful, Dina. As much as people intend for their marriages to last forever, things don't always turn out that way."

Celeste was right, but still, Bertrand's delivery was awful. Not to mention that in his eyes, on paper I looked like some little broken-down girl from the ghetto who needed him to save me. The sad part was, that was exactly where my life was at the moment—in need of saving.

It got me thinking about my assets and what I did and did not have, and it actually made me a bit depressed, because at thirty-one years old, I felt like I should have more to show for myself besides my car, which was a few more months away from being completely paid for, but it wasn't like I drove a Lamborghini. There wasn't much blue book value to a twelve-year-old Honda Accord. Outside of that, I had a small term life insurance policy, which apparently counted as an asset, because it was included in Bertrand's template.

Even with me plugging in the value of my life insurance, my net worth still looked awful, reflecting a negative value. This reality was a huge slap in my face, but I couldn't let Bertrand think I was seriously this broke, so I made up some numbers, inflating the amount of money I had in savings and beefing up my insurance policy values. By the time I was done fudging the numbers, I looked pretty good. All I had to do was explain to Bertrand what was going on with me getting calls from debt collectors. I'd just tell him that there was a certain part of my savings that I never dug into, no matter what. Didn't make much sense to me, but he was so financially disciplined, he might go for it.

With Bertrand's original document now full of red marks where I made corrections to my financial standing, I dialed his number. He answered on the first ring.

"Hey, babe," he said, testing the waters.

"Hi." My voice was intentionally flat and stoic, as I was still feeling some type of way about this whole thing.

"Are you all right?"

"Yeah, I'm fine. I just wanted to talk to you about this . . . this . . . document," I said, unable to get the words *prenuptial agreement* out of my mouth.

"I'm sorry if I offended you, Dina," he immediately blurted.

"No, it's all right. You just caught me off guard," I lied. "I have had a chance to read through it thoroughly, and there are some things on it that need to be changed."

"Okay," he said, more as a question. "Like what?"

"Well, first of all, you didn't have enough financial information on me to complete my portion, so the figures there need correcting."

"Okay," he easily agreed.

"Why did you do it without trying to at least find that information out?"

"Well, I didn't realize that I didn't know any different. I mean, I know you've been talking about the shop being slow for a while, so I knew the salary part was right, and then you shared with me that you were having a hard time making ends meet, so I just assumed that your resources were exhausted."

"For your information, Mr. Bertrand Peyton, I do have other resources. I am just very careful about how I utilize them," I said firmly, delivering my prepared lie.

"I'm sorry. I guess I should have consulted with you first to make sure I had all my facts straight."

"Yes, you should have." I let silence settle for a few seconds as a reprimand, then started speaking again. "Secondly, I want an infidelity clause added in."

"An infidelity clause?"

"Yes."

"What do you propose it states?" he asked.

"I want it to say that if either of us gets caught cheating, as retribution, the injured spouse is owed the value of the current home where we reside, in cash dollars."

"What!" Bertrand sounded just as shocked as I was just a couple of hours ago.

"In other words, if you cheat on me, you owe me the value of the home we live in," I restated.

"What about if you cheat?" he countered, sounding irritated.

"Same thing goes for me. The clause works both ways."

"So let me get this right. You want to move into my house and then try to take it from me?" There was a disbelieving tone to his voice.

"I don't have to move into your house. We can buy a whole new house once we get married if you want to, and no, I'm not trying to take anything. I'm only trying to do what you're trying to do—protect what is important to me."

"How is that?" he questioned.

"Well, clearly, your assets are important to you, which is why you want me to sign a prenup, right?"

"Okay," he said in a "Go on" kind of way.

"What's important to me is my heart, and that's what I want to protect."

"How is you trying to take my house protecting your heart?"

"In my opinion, when you cheat on your spouse, you rob them of a happy home, so that's what you need to replace. There's no peace, love, and happiness inside four walls where someone has violated the marriage vows by cheating. So to make up for ripping away a happy home, the cheater has to replace it with a home that is just as valuable, where the injured spouse can live in peace." Sounded fair to me.

"That's not right!" Bertrand barked.

"Why not?" He was really going to have to explain his point of disagreement to me.

"Because it's not!"

"And if you were to cheat on me, that wouldn't be right, either."

"Why wouldn't you just go back to living in your own apartment? Why would you try to take my house?"

"Again, I am not trying to take anything. I'm only trying to protect what is most important to me. A house can be replaced, money can be remade, sofas and televisions and whatnot can be rebought, but you can't unbreak a heart, and I want to be assured that number one, you won't do that, and number two, if you do, there are consequences for it." I didn't see why he was giving me so much flack on this point.

"So if *you* cheat, then what?"

"I told you, the same thing goes for me. Wherever we live at the time the indiscretion is found out, whatever the value of that particular home is, I'd have to pay you that in cash."

"That doesn't sound right," he huffed.

"Why do you have a problem with it? Are you planning on cheating?"

"It's just not right, Dina," he repeated without answering my question. "I've worked hard for everything that I have, and for you to just try to come in and take it all from me . . ." He trailed off.

"Sounds like you might be a cheater to me."

"It ain't even like that."

"Then what is it like? For me it's no big deal."

"Because you don't have what I have," he retorted.

"And you can keep all your stuff as long as you don't cheat. I don't see where the problem lies."

Bertrand pushed a heavy sigh into my ear. "I gotta think about this one."

"Take your time. I'm not signing this document without that being added."

"That's just like a woman," he mumbled under his breath, but audibly enough for me to hear him.

"Excuse me?"

"I'll get back to you about it."

"Okay. Cool," I stated before he uttered an obligatory "Love you."

"Love you too," I said, almost too jubilantly.

I tossed the document on the floor beside my bed and leaned back on my pillows. *Well played, ma'am. Well played.* The only thing was, I was having serious doubts about moving into his home, but now I couldn't afford not to.

Chapter 10

Candis

I didn't believe in purpose. I didn't believe that people were born to carry out a specific mission in life. I was sick of people asking me, "What's your purpose?" Hell if I knew. I thought that if people were honest, they would admit that it was by happenstance that they'd become who they became. I'd heard too many stories of people saying, "I had no intentions on being a pastor, but God had other plans." Or "When Sister Lettie prophesied over me and told me I was going to be a powerful first lady, I said to myself, 'She didn't hear from God.' But sure enough, here I am." They didn't walk in purpose and destiny and all that crap.

And even for people that had an idea of what they wanted to do and what they wanted to become, that didn't always work out. "I tried my best to be a business owner from the time I was sixteen, but it just didn't work out for me." So I got right irritated when I was sitting in church, minding my own spiritual business, trying to keep my deal with God—although I felt like He played me with that whole Hamilton thing—and the woman on the platform with a wig bigger than her head pointed her finger at me and yelled into the microphone, "You confused because you don't know your purpose!"

I looked around, not realizing who she was talking to, but then she said, "You. Yes, you. Stop looking around, woman in the red blouse." *Oh, snap.* That was indeed me. "You've got to understand your purpose and what you're here for!" she chided. "Stop trying to be in control and do things the way you think they should be done. God knows what He's doing!" she yelled at me in front of the whole congregation. "You sitting up there, trying to direct God in what to do and what to send you, instead of just doing what He's called you to do."

Maybe I *would* do what He's "called" me to do if I knew what it was. But I didn't know, and how would I know? How does anybody know? I wanted to yell that back up there to her, but I knew that wasn't proper church protocol. It kind of made me angry, not so much at her, but at God, because I had been praying and asking Him all kinds of questions about why things weren't working out for me, and He wasn't saying anything. Not a single word. So how was He gonna put me on blast like this in front of all these people, like I hadn't asked Him about this stuff privately?

"Come on up here," the woman demanded. "I'm gonna lay hands on you right now and pray that your eyes be opened and your purpose be revealed!"

People all around me started clapping their hands like I had won some kind of award. I was embarrassed, but I found myself following her instructions and heading for the altar.

"What's your name, sweetheart?"

"Candis," I stated, darting my eyes around me, feeling a thousand pairs of eyeballs burning a hole in the back of my head.

"Lift your hands to the Lord," she instructed further.

Before I had a chance to do that, two female ushers came rushing toward me and stood at my back, I guess preparing to catch me and guide me to the floor if I should happen to faint. They could have kept right on tending to whatever they were doing before I was called up there to be publicly humiliated, because I wasn't about to lie on this floor.

I lifted my hands, and the big-wigged lady slapped my forehead with a greasy hand. As she yelled out some instructions for God to carry out, like, "Open her understanding, Lord," "Show her the way, Lord," "Let the scales fall from her eyes, Lord," her hand violently shook my head back and forth, like she was trying to hurry up and shake salt onto some food. Then she started pushing me backward—I guess to get me to fall back—but like I said, that wasn't gonna happen. I took a step back, and she stepped forward to maintain the pressure on my head. I stepped back again. Then she started yelling, "Don't fight it! Don't fight it! Yield unto the Lord!" The people around me seemed to get louder and louder, praying along with her. This time I stepped back twice, but she pushed harder, charging forth, de-termined not to let me go.

That was when I decided to pray for myself.

God, if you love me at all, even a little bit, please get this woman off my head. Let her go pick on someone else. Please, I'm begging you.

I must have taken about four more steps before she finally eased up off my head by grabbing my hands in-stead. "I'm going to be praying for you, sista. You gotta let it go! You gotta let it go!"

Let what go? What was she talking about? I didn't have anything to hold on to except my sanity. What exactly did she feel I was hoarding? I was silent and tried to look however you were supposed to look when you were being pushed around the church sanctuary in front of a bunch of people. I guess that expression would be respectful, open, and in agreement. Honestly, I felt none of that.

"Ahhhhh!" she uttered, letting out a revealing moan. "You're looking for that man to come a certain way! You got your little checklist ready! Yes, you do. I see it," she said, loud enough for the people down the street and around the corner to hear. "You done told God, 'Send me a man, Lord, but he gotta be this tall and he gotta have this much money and he gotta be this color!' Honey! He ain't coming the way you think he should come. Trust me, you don't want what you think you want! Oh yes! Yeah, yeah, yeah! It was the stone that the builders rejected that became the chief cornerstone. Don't reject your blessing! Don't push it away. He might not look like much on the outside, but there's a blessing in there for you if you dig beneath the surface."

How was that for putting all my business on Front Street? That was what I hated about people doing what church folks called "giving you a word." All your business was just as good as told. I would have tried to leave right then, but my purse was still in the pew where I'd been sitting, not to mention everyone was still staring at me.

As soon as the benediction was over, I grabbed my purse and tried to hightail it to the car, but of course, there were people who felt the need to reach out and pat me on the arm or back with a look of pity on their faces.

"Be encouraged, my sister."

Lord, have mercy. I should have known God would have a trick up His sleeve for me trying to wheel and deal with Him for a man.

Chapter 11

Celeste

I scanned the menu for the cheapest thing listed while Candis and I waited for Dina to arrive. I didn't know why we just couldn't have eaten at Candis's house. She loved to cook and was always throwing some type of social get-together. My wallet sure would have appreciated it. I had only thirty dollars to get me through the next week, and that was before I put gas in the car to get the kids back and forth to school and to job hunt. Being broke was the pits, and being broke but pretending you had enough money to at least have lunch with your girlfriends was even worse.

I'd been out of work for three months now. I couldn't figure out for the life of me why I couldn't nail down another job. I was intelligent, ethical, professional, and I could blow any interview out of the water. I'd chalked it up to the economy, because that was what I heard everyone else blaming their troubles on.

It was only because I had had the sense and discipline to have a little bit of a savings—which Equanto didn't know about—and was able to draw unemployment that we'd not been evicted. I'd also applied for SNAP, or food stamps, as they were called back in the day, to make sure I could feed my babies. I was ashamed to do it, but with three mouths depending on me for breakfast, lunch, and dinner, I had to put pride aside and do what I needed to do.

E had picked up a job at a fast-food joint to fill in the gap, but things weren't that great between us. I was still bitter that he'd gotten me fired from my job. As for the something he needed to take care of that day, it amounted to him going to damn Las Vegas with a couple of his boys, wasting money, and getting drunk. He didn't get back until the next afternoon.

When I told him I'd been fired for being late one too many times, he shook his head and said, "I swear you ain't worth a damn. I told you to catch the bus."

We got to swinging and scrappin' and cussin' and throwing stuff and what have you, but when it was all said and done, I still didn't have a job. And I still had a husband that got on my last nerve every chance he got, but he was my husband, and that was what marriages were made of. Ups and downs, goods and bads, ins and outs, and richer times and poorer times. This was definitely a poorer time, and the last place I needed to be was out at a restaurant, spending money on a meal. I should have just found something else to do at home, but since I wasn't currently working and frequently needed an escape from Equanto, getting together with Candis and Dina had truly become the highlight of my week, so I'd decided to scrape my pennies together and go.

"What can I get you beautiful ladies to drink?" asked our server, a young man who looked like he could be working his way through college. Lawd, I could use a drink right now! I waited to see if Candis ordered an appetizer, and lucky for me, she did.

"I'd like a frozen strawberry daiquiri, and can you bring us the sampler platter please? We're waiting on one more person, but we need something to nibble on," she said.

With appetizers coming, I could skip the entrée and enjoy something other than water to drink. I ordered a drink made of whiskey, peach schnapps, blackberries, mint, fresh-squeezed lemon, and lemon-lime soda. By the time I ate a few chicken fingers and mozzarella sticks, I'd be good.

"How's the job search going, Celeste?" Candis asked.

"Girl, awful. If I don't find something soon, I'm going to need a key to your place," I said in jest, but really, I wasn't kidding. "My savings is getting sucked bone dry."

"At least you had the sense enough to have a savings."

I didn't comment, because truth be told, my savings account was now as empty as a used ziplock bag.

Dina finally made it to the table, looking like she'd had a hard day. "Hey, lovelies," she greeted.

Candis and I answered in unison, while I slid to the left to make room for Dina on my side of the booth.

"I thought you weren't coming," Candis remarked.

"I know. I'm sorry," Dina said, throwing her keys and phone into her purse before she took a seat. "I'm having an emotional day."

"On a Sunday? That's not like you," I commented.

Dina let out a sigh, then responded, "Did you two order yet?"

"Just an appetizer and drinks," Candis stated.

"I wish I knew how to drink. I'd be throwing one back right now," Dina confessed.

I didn't know what Dina could possibly be going through to make her want to drink, but I was sure it didn't compare to the drama I had going on in my own life. Seemed like when your money wasn't right, everything else was out of whack right along with it, including your love life.

I pushed Equanto out of my mind and tried to enjoy my friends.

"So why the long face?" Candis asked.

"I don't want to talk about it right now."

Both Candis and I stared at Dina for a few seconds to make sure that silence was her final answer. When she looked at both of us with a weak smile and a mini shrug, we moved on.

"Well, I've got some news," Candis announced, lifting a chicken finger from the platter and plopping it onto an appetizer plate.

"What? You're pregnant?" I asked. It was my standard response whenever either of them stated they had news to share.

"Gotta be having sex to get pregnant." Candis rolled her eyes.

Dina and I cut our eyes at her, because we both knew good and damn well that Candis was not practicing celibacy.

"Since when did you become a virgin all over again?" I asked before sipping my drink, which was so delicious, it made me flutter my feet under the table. "Mmm!"

"Okay, you're not pregnant, so what's up?" Dina asked between bites of a mozzarella stick.

"I met someone new."

"Who?" I quizzed.

Candis paused, then took a deep breath. She was about to answer, but our server interrupted her.

"You ladies ready to order?"

"I'm good. I'm just gonna snack on this," I rushed to say, motioning with my head to the platter on the table.

Both Candis and Dina ordered something that I thought I might just take a nibble of if they let me.

"So who's the new boyfriend?" I asked.

"First of all, he's not my boyfriend. Secondly, the both of you have to promise not to judge me."

"He must be married," Dina said and guffawed.

"No!" Candis exclaimed, immediately denying it with crinkled brows. "Who wants a married man unless he's *your* married man? Been there, done that, and once was enough."

"Whose husband were you sleeping with?" Dina said with a gasp. That was news to me too, and Candis and I had been friends for years.

"I don't even want to think about it. That was the worst thing I've ever done," she answered, shaking her head. "Anyway, he's not really new. I've kind of told y'all about him already."

"Who is it? That SeanMichael dude?" Dina asked.

Candis bounced her eyes between us before she answered, "Yeah."

Dina shrugged. "What's the big deal about that? You've been talking to him for what? Like two or three months now?"

"Yeah, but that's not the part I need to tell you about."

"Then what is it?" I sipped more of my drink, starting to enjoy a buzz.

"We met online."

"Like on one of those matchmaking sites?" Dina asked.

Candis shook her head. "Not exactly."

Dina and I didn't say another word, waiting for her to spill it.

"We met on Facebook."

"Facebook? What are you? Sixteen?" I laughed, not taking her seriously.

"I said, 'Don't judge me,'" Candis reminded us, pointing at us with the tines of her fork. I stuffed more food in my mouth to keep myself from saying anything more, but my lifted eyebrows let her know that I was indeed judging.

"Are you serious?" Dina asked, looking for some sign of a joke.

"Yep." Candis didn't crack a smile. In fact, her pursed lips and slightly raised brows signaled her honesty.

"Humph." I commented. "You must not watch Lifetime. What was that movie that they showed not too long ago? The murderer from Craigslist or something?"

"*The Craigslist Killer,*" Dina corrected.

I nodded. "Yeah, that."

"Cut it out," Candis begged. "You two are the only ones I can share this with."

"So what do you know about him?" I asked after a bit of a pause, which meant we'd try not to give our opinions on how dangerous an online-sparked romance could be.

"What are his statistics?" Dina threw in, looking at Candis dead on.

"He's thirty-two, no kids, likes music, kinda looks like Brian McKnight." Candis blushed as she stirred her drink with a straw, watching the ripples it made in her glass with a dreamy stare.

"Where does he live? You've been to his house already?" I shot back.

"No." Her grin faded into a more apprehensive expression. "Promise y'all won't trip when I tell you where he lives."

"Just the fact that you are telling us not to trip automatically means we're gonna trip. You do realize that, right?" I responded with raised brows.

"Oh, Lawd, he's in jail!" Dina blurted out, assuming the worst.

"He is not!"

"The halfway house?" Dina asked, guessing again.

Candis shook her head. "No. Inmates don't have Facebook privileges."

"Then it must be with his momma," I concluded before sipping my drink.

"No. He lives in Maryland," Candis revealed.

Both Dina and I stared at Candis stoically, waiting for her to tell us more.

"Maryland?" Dina asked to confirm.

"Yes."

"Maryland, like the state? Over on the East Coast, near Washington, D.C.?" I asked. "Where the president of the United States runs the country from?"

Candis nodded. "Yes, the state."

"Girl, I thought you'd met somebody." I dismissed her notion with an indifferent wave. "Quit playing."

"I'm serious. I mean, we haven't met physically, but we are talking." She paused for a few seconds. "Well, actually, we're officially a couple."

Dina didn't respond. She was busy checking in with Bertrand via text for the third time since we'd been there.

"That's like dating a ghost, Candis," I said, rolling my eyes to the ceiling.

"It's not like dating a ghost. It's called a long-distance relationship," she said, trying to defend herself.

"Most long-distance relationships start when the two people at least see each other face-to-face first and *then* one of them moves away," I retorted. "You ain't never seen this man. That ain't no long-distance relationship. That's a hot mess waiting to happen."

"Is it different than the hot mess you have happening in your home?" she shot at me, but those bullets bounced right off, as if I were made of rubber.

"A hot mess is a hot mess, and just because I got one, don't mean you have to get one too. My last name ain't Jones. You don't have to keep up with me."

Candis fell silent, and I nudged her under the table to look at Dina, whose facial expression had switched from one that indicated she was having a good time with her girls to one that said Bertrand was getting on her last nerve.

"What's wrong with you, Dina?" I asked.

She turned her lips down and shook her head from side to side. "Nothing. I'll be right back." She slid out of the booth and stayed gone for fifteen minutes, and when she came back, it looked like she'd been crying.

Bertrand was taking her ass through hell. What kind of hell, it was hard to say, but I lived in hell every day at my house, and I knew full well what it looked like.

Chapter 12

Dina

Bertrand had been crazy upset the day before, when I'd texted him from the restaurant to let him know I was having lunch with Candis and Celeste, instead of spending the afternoon with him. I couldn't even half get into the conversation about Candis and this new cross-country boyfriend due to him blowing my phone up with a thousand questions and complaints. At one point I had to get up and leave the table to call him.

"So why didn't I get invited to lunch?" he'd grumbled into the phone.

"Because it's our girls' luncheon, babe," I'd said calmly, standing in front of the restaurant.

"So you're out, going to places where your man can't come."

"Bertrand, it's me, Candis, and Celeste. It's not that you *can't* come. It's just our girlfriend time together. You are not one of our girlfriends. Why would you *want* to come?" He hated for me to spend time with other people, and I hated that he hated that.

"To be with you," he stated in a tone that suggested I should have been able to draw that conclusion on my own.

"To be with me or to keep tabs on me?" I challenged, becoming angry.

"Well, how do I know that you are where you say you are?"

"Why would you think I was lying?" I practically screamed.

"I just ain't never seen someone having a problem with their man wanting to spend time with them. Most women gotta beg for time from their man. Something just don't sound right. That's all I'm saying."

"Well, you're just going to have to learn to trust me, Bertrand. I'm going back to lunch."

I didn't mention it to Dina and Celeste, but I'd actually seen Bertrand drive through the restaurant's parking lot yesterday, while we ate and talked. It made my stomach turn. I couldn't help but keep looking around to see if he was going to pop up at our table. He never did. I guess seeing my car in the lot was proof enough. Or maybe he peeked around the corner to see who I was with, and I just didn't see him. When I got home, I was still steamed, but he seemed to be content, like nothing had ever happened.

I'd just pulled some grilled teriyaki wings from the oven, whipped up some homemade mashed potatoes, and made bacon-wrapped asparagus when Bertrand walked in the door from work.

"Look at you! You got it smelling all good in here!" he commented, walking over to the stove and pulling me into his arms as he grinned at the cooked food. "You gonna mess around and make me marry you." Our lips met in a standard kiss, but it evolved into one that promised that after dinner, there'd be flesh-flavored dessert. He tightened his arms around me in a hug that emanated love. "I'm so glad you're here," he whispered. "This feels good."

"What does?"

"Coming home to someone waiting for me. Coming home to a beautiful"—he stopped to peck my lips between each of his next words—"gorgeous, sexy, smart, incredible, amazing future wife." With one arm wrapped around my waist, he took my right hand into his left and started swaying to some inaudible music. "I can't wait to marry you," he whispered.

We hadn't talked any more about moving forward with the wedding in the past two months, even though I'd comfortably moved into his home. It was our very own elephant that lurked around, peeking around corners when it felt like it, like it had just done. I hadn't changed my mind about wanting that extra line added to the so-called prenup, and he wasn't acting like he planned to add it, so it looked like, for all intents and purposes, the wedding was on hold.

Ignoring the elephant, like we'd done for eight straight weeks now, I returned his sentiment with, "I can't wait to marry you, either, babe." In some place in my heart, I meant it. Bertrand was good to me. We didn't always agree on everything, but he loved me and I knew that. "So what's taking you so long?" I added.

"I'm waiting on you," he mumbled. By that, he probably meant he was waiting on me to sign my name on that paper.

"I'm ready right now," I teased.

"Let's go then."

We kissed and broke our embrace, both knowing we weren't going to go anywhere but to bed and our conversation on tying the knot would be put on the shelf until next time.

"Sit down and let me serve you." I pushed Bertrand toward the table.

"Let me just wash my hands first."

I piled food on our plates, sat them on the table, then poured two glasses of sparkling lemonade, took a seat, and waited for Bertrand to return. It seemed to be taking him forever.

"Babe!" I yelled from the kitchen.

"Yeah?" he called back.

"What are you doing? Your food is getting cold." And I was ready to eat.

"I'm coming. Wait a minute."

Curious, I got up from the table and trekked toward the bedroom but found him sitting at his desk in his home office. "What are you doing?" I asked a second time, wondering what had his attention.

"Just balancing my checkbook."

"You have to do that now? I thought we were going to have dinner."

"We are, babe. Just give me a few minutes to get this done," he said, keeping his focus on his physical checkbook and his computer monitor, which displayed his online checking account.

"All right." I turned and went back to the table, but when Bertrand still hadn't made it back after ten minutes, I started getting frustrated. "Babe, come eat!" I yelled down the hallway.

"I'm coming!" he called, his voice echoing.

I was trying not to be petty, but I went through the effort of trying to have a hot meal on the table for him, and now it was stone cold. The food being cold didn't bother me as much as the fact that he seemed not to care about it. I didn't know a man that didn't make his way to the table to eat once the dinner bell was rung. After another ten minutes went by, I was done waiting. Shoving my plate in the microwave, I brought my food back up to an acceptable temperature, then took it in the den, plopped on the couch, and ate in front of the TV, just like I would have done if I were still in my apartment. I was halfway done eating when Bertrand finally came back.

"You couldn't wait for me?" he asked, his tone suggesting surprise and annoyance.

"Tried to," I answered without looking up.

"I told you I was coming."

"You were taking too long." I shrugged. "Your food's been on the table for thirty, thirty-five minutes now."

"I thought we were going to eat together," he stated, sounding a bit irritated.

"So did I. You refused to come to the table." I was just as irritated as he was.

He stood silent, watching me as I forked more food in my mouth, then shook his head and walked out. I thought he was headed to the kitchen to warm his plate and join me in the den, but instead he walked out the front door.

I sat my almost finished plate on the coffee table, quickly washed my hands, and rushed to the door to see where he was headed. Surprisingly, he hadn't gone far. He was sitting on the front porch, looking pensive and upset.

"What's wrong with you?"

"Nothing," he uttered.

"Why are you sitting outside?"

"Just needed some air."

I stared at him the same way he'd been staring at me just a few minutes before. He couldn't be trippin' because I ate without him.

"Your food is on the table," I reminded him. "It's good too!"

"I'll get it later."

"You're mad at me?"

He shook his head. "I don't think *mad* is the word."

"You're upset?"

"I guess I'm just a little disappointed," he answered, turning his head toward me.

"Disappointed in what?"

"I just thought that you would wait for me."

"How long was I supposed to wait, Bertrand? Until you felt like coming?"

He didn't answer.

"And I thought that you would appreciate me cooking so much that you would sit down and eat, so I guess I'm disappointed too, but it's no big deal." This was silly. "Your food is still in there, and I'm still here"—I shrugged—"so what's the problem?"

Bertrand remained silent and looked out into the yard. After a few seconds, he shook his head. "There's no problem."

Rolling my eyes and turning on my heels, I bounced back in the house, finished my food, and washed the dishes. I was cleaning off the stove and countertops when Bertrand came back inside. Without saying a word, he grabbed some plastic wrap from the pantry closet, covered his plate with the clear film, sat it in the refrigerator, and headed to the bedroom. By the time I finished the kitchen and did some general straightening up in the other rooms, Bertrand had showered and turned in for bed, and when I tried to nestle up to him, naked and ready, he stiff-armed me.

Chapter 13

Dina

All I was doing was putting away the laundry. I'd not had any appointments for the past three days, and I couldn't just sit around the house, doing nothing. Since I was all set up to be Bertrand's wife, it wasn't crazy that I'd be doing stuff that a housewife would do . . . like cooking meals and washing clothes. So honestly, that was what I was doing. Okay. I was snooping. Well, I was doing a little bit of both. But Bertrand didn't have to know that.

I opened his drawer to put away a stack of T-shirts. Usually, I just folded the laundry and let Bertrand put his own things away, but not this day. I called it doing a little extra, which included looking through the entire drawer. And that was when I found them. A pair of baby blue French-cut panties that didn't belong to me, nicely folded and wedged between two T-shirts. I stared at them for two minutes, wondering what the hell they were doing there. Who did these panties belong to? How long had they been there? Was this man cheating on me? And now what was I going to do? If I asked him about it and he was seeing someone else, he would only lie about it. And if he wasn't seeing anyone, I didn't know that I would believe him.

I did go through every single drawer, looking for whatever else was there. I didn't find anything else that looked suspicious, but that one pair of panties was enough. But what was it enough for? Enough to make me leave him? Enough to ruin our relationship? That all depended on how he reacted when I confronted him.

It was only four in the morning when my body decided I'd had enough sleep. Although I tried to go back to sleep so I wouldn't be bombarded with my thoughts, the sandman had apparently finished his rounds and wasn't working a second shift. Although fully awake, I tossed and turned, and Bertrand began to stir.

"What's wrong, babe?" he mumbled.

"I can't sleep." I guess his interpretation of that was I was horny, because he grabbed my hand and placed it on his groin. I hid my sigh, and I was really going to try to get my mind together to have sex, but I couldn't do it, knowing what I knew. I withdrew my hand after only a few seconds of fondling.

"What's wrong?" he asked.

"We need to talk," I began. That was the only thing I could come up with.

Bertrand sighed a sleepy sigh first, then replied, "About what?"

Without notice, I reached for the lamp on the nightstand and clicked the light on, blinding both of us momentarily.

"You need to turn on the light?" he asked, wincing.

"Yeah, because I need to see your face, and I'm going to need your full attention."

I waited for him to pull his hand away from his eyes, and though he had them scrunched into narrow slits, he looked at me. "What is it?"

A sigh preceded my next actions, which were pulling myself out of bed, walking over to the chest of drawers that held his clothes, opening the third one from the top, and pulling out the pair of panties that were not mine.

"Why are these in your drawer?" I asked, holding them up with just a pinch of my nails.

"What is it?" he huffed, his voice still heavy with sleep.

I flung the panties at him, and they landed on his chest. Bertrand glanced down at them, then casually picked them up.

"They yours, babe," he said with crinkled brows.

"If they were mine, I wouldn't be asking you about them." I paused, studying his face. He looked both confused and upset. "So whose are they?"

"What do you mean? You're the only woman that lives here. They gotta be yours."

"But they are not, and they are in your drawer. So whose are they?" I asked again.

"Babe, you waking me up in the middle of the night to ask me about some underwear?" He sighed and let his eyes scan the ceiling, as if the answer would be found imprinted above his head. "I don't know."

"Yes, you do," I insisted. "They didn't just appear there by themselves."

"They probably been there for I don't know how long," he said. "I haven't been through those drawers to clean stuff out of them."

"So you're trying to tell me these are Miranda's stank drawers," I said, referencing the woman he'd dated before we started dating. I instantly regretted giving him a possible answer. "What are you doing? Holding on to them for old times' sake?"

"No, I'm not holding on to them," he said, defending himself.

"So what are they doing here? Still. We've been together for a whole year now, and you mean to tell me that you at no point in time saw those nasty panties in your drawer, in the bedroom where you and your future wife sleep, and you haven't thought enough to throw them out?"

"I just told you, I haven't been through those drawers. I don't know all of what is in there."

"So you didn't think enough of me to clean up your old mess before I moved in here with you?"

"Not really. I had no idea they were there," he said.

I wasn't appeased.

"Those things are as old as dirt."

This felt like some cheating Cameron garbage all over again. But suppose he was telling the truth? Maybe they were old and were just some leftovers, but still I shouldn't have found them. I didn't know what to say at that point, not knowing if I should accept his story or not.

"Babe. I promise you, it's nothing." He threw the covers off his body while grabbing the underwear and put them in a small wastebasket across the room.

"Don't you think you need to be taking that mess outside?" My hands were on my hips as I shot invisible daggers from my eyes.

Bertrand sighed loudly but didn't say a word. He pulled on a pair of shorts that were draped across the chaise, grabbed the panties from the trash, and left the bedroom, me trailing just a few feet behind him. I followed him to the back door, and seconds after he stepped outside, I heard the rumbling of the trash receptacle. When Bertrand came back in, I was still standing there with my arms folded across my chest. He walked past me, back into our bedroom, removed his shorts, and got back in bed without saying a single word.

I stood just inside our bedroom with my arms still folded, but with nothing to say, staring at him. After a full minute went by, he rolled to my side of the bed and turned out the light, leaving me standing in the dark. "You coming back to bed?" he asked, as if nothing had happened.

That made me angry. He acted like it should have been over, but I wasn't ready for it to be over.

"How do you expect me just to jump right back in the bed with you when you've been saving some woman's drawers for a souvenir!" I blurted.

"I wasn't saving them, Dina," he said calmly as he rolled over and punched his pillow for comfort. "I told you, I didn't realize they were there. They are outside in the trash now. That's it. It's over. It's done."

"How do you think it's done? I find some wench's underwear in your drawer, and just because you put them outside, it's over? All she's gonna do is give you another pair."

"Dina, you're being ridiculous."

"Oh, so if you find some boxers over in my drawers that don't belong to you, you're going to be okay with that?" I argued. "That's not going to be an issue for you?"

"Babe, what's really wrong?"

"What do you mean, what's wrong?" I fired back. "You don't see nothing wrong with you having them here in the first place?"

"Of course I do," he responded. "But they are gone now, and that's the most I can do about it. If I had known they were in there earlier, I would have thrown them out. I didn't know. Now they're gone. Can we go back to sleep now? Because I have to be up for work in just a couple of hours."

I wanted to say something more, but what could be said? He was right. The issue was resolved for the most part. But only if I chose to believe what he'd just told me, as I had no way of knowing how long those panties had been there, since I'd never actually gone through his drawers before. I couldn't even say what prompted me to go through his drawers this time. Just curiosity, I guess. Now that I seemed to have found and opened Pandora's box, I didn't know what to do.

Chapter 14

Celeste

At long last, I was able to start work again. It was only at the grocery store, but something was better than nothing, and I wasn't going to look a gift horse in the mouth. It was different from my receptionist job, where I got to sit on my butt all day, manage my personal life between my tasks, answer my cell and text messages if I needed or wanted to, and even catch up on some reading when it was slow. Being a cashier didn't afford me any of that. I was on my feet for the entire shift, scanning food and collecting money. Even when it was slow, we had to do what was called re-shop, which meant putting back any groceries that customers had left at the register for one reason or another. With all this extra weight on me, by the time I got off from a six- or seven-hour shift, I was dog tired, my feet ached, and I didn't feel like dealing with any of Equanto's craziness.

Every day it was the same old thing. Either we were arguing about money, him keeping a job, and his disappearing acts, or we weren't speaking at all. It wasn't a good environment for my kids to be in, and I would often wish I had somewhere else to go. Anywhere. One of the things that kept me holding on, though, was that I didn't want to be judged by my friends, who'd never thought very much of Equanto in the first place. One thing that no one wanted to hear was, "I told you so." And every couple had to deal with drama at some point in their marriage, so really, what E and I were going through was probably no different than anyone else's marriage.

Luckily, I was able to get a morning shift, so the kids were in school while I worked, and I generally got home forty-five minutes before they did. A lot of times, I'd just sit out in the car instead of going inside the house, because it was the only place between work and home where I could find peace and could have a moment to myself. Some days I'd listen to music, other days I made phone calls, and then some days I sat in total silence, wondering why I'd done this to myself and praying for a way out that wouldn't embarrass me. It was in those silent sessions that I couldn't stop the tears from flowing down my face once they started.

The simple fact of the matter was my husband didn't love me. He never had. I was mad at myself for accepting him into my life by marrying him, then tying him to me forever by getting pregnant twice. I guess I was looking for love at any cost but never recognized that love existed in our relationship only on my side. Even though I was the mother of his children, it was obvious that he had no love for me, and that broke my heart every day. Equanto was forever putting me down and calling me names, and I tried to act like it didn't bother me, but in all honesty, it tore at my soul every single time.

I felt like I worked hard for my family and at taking care of my children. The boys were clean, well fed— even if it meant exposing my entire life story to the people at the food stamp office—healthy, and smart. I cooked practically every day and kept the house tidy. Even with Equanto constantly hurling insults at me and hurting my feelings whenever he felt like it, my legs were always open to him whenever he wanted a little nooky. The few times I did turn him down, he went on a verbal tirade.

"Whatchu mean, you don't feel like it? You better be glad somebody wants your fat ass. Who you think gone want you but me? I can't even hardly look at you. Cut the damn light off 'fore you give me nightmares."

His words cut like a knife, and I must have cried that whole night the first time he said that. Mostly because I believed it. Didn't nobody else want me, else I wouldn't have ended up with his ass. My phone wasn't ringing off the hook with relationship choices when I met Equanto. That was why I was on the love chat line in the first place, looking for someone to love me. And maybe someone would have if I didn't like to eat so much and my butt—and various other parts of me—wasn't so big.

I knew that my weight was one thing that I had complete control over. All I had to do was start making some healthy eating choices and, instead of sitting in this car every day for almost an hour, take a walk around the block a few times. It would be a start. I just wasn't motivated to do it. I tried a couple of times, but as soon as Equanto got to cussin' and calling me fat and creating drama, I knew where to get a little piece of sunshine, and many times it came with the name Little Debbie, Tastykake, or Edy's on it since I was now working at the grocery store.

In my rearview mirror, I could see the boys getting off the school bus and racing each other to the car. They'd come to expect me to be sitting there, waiting. After the first week or two of finding me there, they just started getting inside the car and sitting with me. Even on the days when there wasn't enough gas in the car to run the air-conditioning and it was just as hot as LL Cool J said he was in his "Rock the Bells" lyrics.

"Hey, Mom!" they greeted one at a time.

"Hey, babies. Tell me about your school day," I requested and got ready to listen to each one of them share every detail of what they had experienced in the last eight hours. I made sure to listen intently, even on the days when a splitting headache made me wish they didn't have so much to say. I wanted my boys to know that what they had to say and share was important to me.

This particular day, once they got in the car, instead of sitting there, I cranked it up and pulled out of the lot.

"Where are we going, Mom?" Linwood asked.

"I'm taking you boys to get ice cream cones."

"Yea!" they cheered.

It had been a while since I'd been able to treat the boys to much of anything, and today was just as good a day as any, since I'd just gotten paid. I could have used my food stamp card just as easily to buy ice cream at the grocery store, but a change of scenery would do us all some good.

We'd gotten our cones and taken a seat at a table in the dining room of the restaurant when my youngest boy, Jerrod, hit me with question that felt like a brick slamming against my head.

"Mommy, does Daddy love you?"

"Yeah," I said without hesitation, but it didn't even sound right coming out of my mouth. "What made you ask that?"

"Because he always be mean to you, and I thought when you love somebody, you supposed to treat them nice."

"Well, you are," I confirmed.

"Daddy don't never be nice to you. I don't think he love you," Jerrod declared.

"Nice like what? What do you think he should be doing?"

"Like kissing you and hugging you and giving you flowers and, like, some lollipops or something."

"Is that what you're going to do when you get a girlfriend?" I asked, embarrassed that my baby had recognized that my and Equanto's marriage was dysfunctional, to say the least.

"Yep! I'm not going to be nothing like Daddy. I'm going to give my girlfriend Now-Laters and fruit snacks," he announced.

"You better not be kissing her," I teased.

"I'm just gonna kiss her on the cheek, 'cause you supposed to wait 'til you married before you kiss someone on the lips," Jerrod replied.

His brothers laughed at him, not that they knew any better.

"You and Daddy don't never kiss," Quincy added.

"Just because you don't see us kissing, that doesn't mean we don't kiss," I said.

"How about holding hands?" Jerrod asked.

"We really are too busy to hold hands, Jerrod."

"I'ma hold my girlfriend's hand too."

"You sure got a lot of girlfriend plans. How old do you plan on being when you get this girlfriend?"

"I don't know." Jerrod shrugged as he licked his cone. "I think about twenty-seven."

He made me laugh. "Oh, okay."

"Do you love Daddy?" he asked next.

"Of course I do."

"Oh. I'm glad I asked, 'cause I didn't know. Y'all don't act like it."

Ouch.

Chapter 15

Dina

I don't care who you are, where you come from, and how good you can work your goody box. If you are a woman who's ever been in a relationship, you've been cheated on. And what I want to know is, why is it that heffas think that just because ten years passed by, you've forgotten all about the time they slept with your man, and then they wanna be grinnin' in your face like the two of you are best friends? I wanted to punch Vanisha Yarborough dead in the jaw when I saw her earlier today. I was stopping by the grocery store to pick up a cup of yogurt on my way to church, and she spotted me from across the parking lot.

"Dina!" she called.

I looked up and saw her getting out of her car, but I didn't have my glasses on to readily identify her, not that that would have made a whole lot of difference. Since I'd done some of everybody's hair in Laveen, I was thinking she could have been some potential business, which I needed desperately, so I waited the few seconds it took for her to come into focus.

"Dammit!" I mumbled under my breath once I realized who it was.

"Girl, how you doing?" She grinned, showing every tooth she had, and a few that she didn't.

"Hey, Vanisha." I gave a half smile, like I'd let by-gones be bygones, but just like that, I felt disdain bubbling in my stomach, wanting to turn into spit and be hurled out of my mouth toward her. The Christian part of me fought against it and won. Even if I wasn't a Christian, I didn't think I could ever spit in somebody's face.

"You look good!" she commented, circling me with her eyes. I refrained from rolling mine.

"Thanks."

"So what're you doing now? How's Cameron?"

I didn't care that Cameron and I were no longer together, but I still couldn't appreciate what the two of them did behind my back, and practically in my face.

"I have no idea." I shrugged. "Look, I'm in a bit of a rush. I'm trying to get to church on time," I said, digging in my purse for nothing in particular, but it made me look busy and in a rush.

"Oh, okay! Don't let me hold you, then! Look me up on Facebook so we can catch up!" She backed away from me, then headed toward another store in the strip mall.

"All right, girl. Take care," I said for the sake of being cordial. If only I had the boldness and brashness to cuss her out. It didn't matter that her offenses were a decade old.

Seeing Vanisha wrecked my morning mood. As soon as you purpose in your heart that you're going to have a good day, no matter what, here comes the devil with some foolishness to make you regret getting out of bed at all. I made my way through the store and paid for my items, wishing again that I'd had the boldness to cuss Vanisha out. Getting back in my car, I tried to refocus on having a great day, but my mind had a mind of its own and traveled back ten years, to when I was young, dumb, naive, and so in love with Cameron, I didn't believe he had a fault anywhere in his being. And like a blinded fool, I ignored what was right in front of me. Vanisha and I had been friends all through high school, with me envying her style, her smile, and her charismatic personality. I didn't know how we got to be friends, because she was one of those fast-tailed girls who'd made a name for herself by having sex with various boys after school, and sometimes during school, when she skipped classes. I, on the other hand, wasn't interested in having sex with anybody, but I found her taboo adventures interesting and exciting.

"Girl, he got a big ol' dick," she'd told me about so many of the boys we went to school with—just pick a name. "We stayed after yesterday and did it in the girls' locker room in the ninth-grade gym."

"For real?" I'd asked the first time she said that to me. My eyes had to be stretched as big as the moon. "What does it feel like, though?"

She'd jerked her head back like I was asking the most asinine question in the world. "It feels good!"

I didn't know how to interpret that, and I wasn't ready to find out for myself, so I'd have to take her word for it. By the time we graduated, she'd had more sex partners than my momma had years of her life.

Even with me knowing how loose she was, I thought our friendship was stronger than her promiscuity, so I had no problem with her meeting and knowing about Cameron. I'd met Cameron when I was eighteen, while walking home from Vanisha's house after she had spent eight hours braiding my hair. He was hot and sweaty from chasing a basketball around on the court, but he seemed delighted to make my acquaintance in passing. We hit it off right away, and I found him adorably sweet, handsome, and respectful. After a couple months of dating, we were inseparable when he wasn't in class. I gave that man my heart, my soul, the very essence of my womanhood. And he graciously and gently took it. It wasn't long before I got pregnant, and although we were young, we decided marriage was the right thing to do.

Vanisha was the maid of honor at my wedding, stood right there staring at my coochie when I gave birth to my baby girl, Tiara, and held my hand when I couldn't stop crying after Tiara's underdeveloped lungs wouldn't allow her to live past two days. Vanisha was my homegirl, my sista friend, my ace boon coon.

Before I turned twenty, Cameron and I had an apartment, struggled with consumer debt, and had scarred credit from trying to pay off the hospital bill from the baby we'd had and lost without having insurance. Cameron ended up dropping out of college to work full-time as an employee of Anheuser-Busch, while I tried to get my cosmetologist career off the ground. It wasn't the best life, but I was happy being Mrs. Cameron Allen.

Now here was where I started messing up. See, Cameron was my first. All I'd learned about sex, or what I thought sex should be, I learned from Vanisha's explicit stories, erotica books, movie scenes, and misogynistic videos of girls shaking their booties on the BET channel. My mother was far too prudish to have any real sex conversations with me, other than giving me instructions to keep my panties up.

Like every woman before me who'd opened her legs for the man she loved, I wanted to sex him out of his mind. From what I'd seen on videos and such, I was expecting a certain reaction out of Cameron. I wanted to hear some "Oohs" and "Aahs," some "Oh, babies" and "Oh, my Gods!" I wanted to see his face contort uncontrollably and hear a series of cuss words leave his lips before he collapsed in a heap on top of me, panting, "Damn, Dina girl!" But most times when Cameron and I made love, he was silent and rhythmic—never calling my name, never losing himself in a series of gasps, never having to catch his breath. His expression always looked stoic and disengaged, nothing like I'd seen on TV.

I tried to provoke a response from him by adding my own sound effects, moaning his name to stroke his ego, although honestly, I didn't really *feel* anything to make me do that. Nonetheless, I thought if I made him believe he was puttin' it down, it would make him more responsive. Well, it didn't work, and when it didn't, what did my stupid behind do? I asked Vanisha for some sex tips.

"I don't know what I'm doing wrong," I complained one day, standing in the middle of her apartment, dancing to videos. "He just seems like he doesn't enjoy it."

"Girl, you gotta know how to work that thang!" she said and laughed, twisting a single leg in a circular motion and rotating her hips in a way that could probably make her some money if she were in a strip joint. "I mean, what do you be doing?"

I shrugged. "What you mean?"

"You don't just be lying there like a board, do you?"

"No," I answered, embarrassed. "I be into it, moving and stuff," I said, trying to defend myself. "But it's like . . ." I shrugged again. "I don't know . . . like he's bored or something."

"Humph! I don't know what kinda sex y'all be having that he be acting bored," she said. "Do you be going down on him?" she asked, just as easily as if she were asking for a stick of chewing gum.

"I mean, I . . . we . . ." I didn't know how to answer that question. I was ashamed to admit that I'd put my husband's thing-a-ling in my mouth, but at the same time, I was ashamed to say that I hadn't.

"Maybe you need to do that," she commented when I couldn't get any words to come out of my mouth. "Girl, men love that." She grinned and nodded. "If that don't make him cuss, you're definitely doing something wrong."

It wasn't long after that conversation that all of a sudden Vanisha started coming over all the damn time. "Girl, I was just dropping by. I don't want nothing," she'd say. "You mind if I do a load of laundry over here at your house? My washer won't spin. My air conditioner broke down again. I had to come over here just so I could cool off a little bit."

I, being the unsuspecting dummy that I was back then, let her conniving ass come right on in. And like a vulture waiting for a wild animal to die, she circled a few times, then came in for a landing—right in my and Cameron's bed. I never actually caught them doing the do, and I guess that was why I ignored what was right in front of me—believing that Cameron could and would make love only to me. I trusted him; I trusted her. When I became suspicious for obvious reasons and questioned Cameron about it, he did what all men did, denied and lied.

Cameron made up outrageous stories about how he was supposed to be at work but ended up at her house first because she'd called, asking for a jump. And how he was just sitting at home, minding his business, while I was out getting a pedicure, when she came over, asking if she could take a shower at our house, because her water got cut off. And how . . . Well, I don't want to think about it anymore, but let's just say my momma raised a damn fool. Except I didn't realize it then like I did now.

I'd never realized until today just how hurt I still was over the thought that Cameron had screwed another woman, my best friend at that. I also realized how much I hated her and Cameron for it. I thought I had let that mess go, especially after Cameron and I divorced. We parted ways for a number of reasons—she happened not to be one of them—because, like I said, I was too stupid to trust and act on what I innately knew. Now here I was, with a cup of yogurt and a bottle of orange juice in my hands, headed to the house of the Lord with a heart full of hate.

"Work on me, Jesus," I whispered as a prayer, "because I don't want to hate anybody, but I don't know how to get rid of that hurt from this betrayal." "Help me Lord," I added, because tears were now welling in my eyes. Not specifically because of my recollections of Vanisha and Cameron, but because of the panties that I'd found tucked in Bertrand's drawer the other week, and because I was wondering whether I was being a fool all over again.

The next day, I just couldn't hold myself together. I tried to, but every little thing made me cry. Ms. Maybelle, a nasty old bat of a woman whose hair I'd been doing every Tuesday for the past six years, took notice of my less than pleasant demeanor and knew that this time she wasn't the cause of it. She then did something she'd never done before: with a heart filled with compassion, she asked me what was wrong.

"Looks like something bothering you, baby. What's going on?" she asked while I pressed her hair.

"I'm all right, Ms. Maybelle. Just got a lot on my mind."

"Naw, naw, naw. It's something more than that," she responded intuitively. "What is it? Go on and share your heart."

I was reluctant at first, but what did I have to lose by sharing with this woman, who had one foot in the grave and the other on a banana peel? Wasn't like she could run out and tell it to anyone that would matter.

"My fiancé and I are just going through a rough time," I said, wringing my hands. Suddenly I felt like a schoolgirl, trying to explain some misbehavior to my teacher.

"Every relationship have problems, baby. Every one of 'em. Ain't a single one out there where somebody ain't been taken to hell. I been married three times in my lifetime, and each time I just knew I was setting myself up for the best possible life. Let me tell you, honey, ain't na' one of my husbands ever done completely right by me."

That was disheartening to hear.

"He ain't beatin' you, is he?" she asked.

"No, ma'am." I instantly shook my head.

"I ain't think so. Ain't never seen you come up in here with no bumps and bruises. So he must be tippin' on the side. That's the only other thing that will break a woman down like you is broke down right now."

My silence said what I couldn't bring my mouth to say. The panties were bad enough, but after that, I found a few text messages that made me even more suspicious, although they weren't exactly incriminating.

"Let me tell you something. Everybody cheat, everybody," she stated adamantly, looking me in the eye.

I was no cheater, but I did have my moments of wondering what different men would be like in bed. That was as far as I ever took it, though.

"You just have to find the one that takes care of home and respects you that you can tolerate. You ain't gone escape that cheatin' thang, no matter what you do. Now, if you can put up with your future husband, gone and put up with him. Otherwise, you gonna end up alone and lonely and bitter something terrible. Then you gone be forever searching for that one person who you thank gone do you right. Save yourself some time, sugar. He ain't out there. He just ain't."

"Yes, ma'am," I answered, but not because I fully agreed with her. But it seemed appropriate to say that.

"You gone have to learn how to get over it and stop crying over spilled milk. I know it hurt, 'cause I been there. Now, if you just cain't put it past you and get over it, then you gotsta make a decision. You hear me?"

"Yes, ma'am," I answered again.

"If you cain't live with him in peace, then you get up and leave his sorry ass. Ain't no sense in living miserable for the rest of your life. Then, when you dead and gone, that same man gone be sitting there at your funeral, telling everybody how he would do anything to get you back, when truth be told, he the one that ran you to your grave in the first place. And guess where all them no-good skanks he done slept with gone be? They gone be somewhere nearby, just waiting for them to drop you in the ground so they can drop their drawers for him again. I'm telling you what I know. I done seen it happen time and time again."

"Yes, ma'am."

"Now, I been watching you come up in here for the past month with your face all long and drawn out, looking right pitiful, and I know what that look mean." She paused and studied my face for a few seconds. "I know what it mean. Done seen it too many times before. Now what you gotta do is ask yourself if you got any strength left."

She stared directly into my eyes, demanding an answer, but I kept quiet, because honestly, I didn't know.

"Well, do you?"

"I . . . I think so."

"Chile, you don't know your own strength. You know you ain't got to put up with no man and his bullshit." Hearing her cuss made me giggle. "You gone and get yourself together and move on and have yourself a happy life. Don't you think you deserve to be happy?"

"Yes."

"So what you sittin' round for? Gone and be happy. Be happy with him, or be happy without him. If he taking good care of you and paying the bills like he supposed to be doing, let him go on, and you find you a little something on the side."

All right, she was going a bit too far by suggesting that I start cheating on my man just to balance things out. I just didn't have it in me to do that. I'd leave him before I'd cheat.

"What's good for the goose is good for the gander. You make sure you remember that, hear?"

"But what about love, Ms. Maybelle?"

"Chile, love is overrated. It don't put money in the bank or pay no damn bills." She went on for a few more minutes, then ended her speech with, "Now, fix your face and gone and curl my hair. I got somewhere to be after a while."

While I flipped and rolled my Marcel irons through her hair, I mulled over everything she'd said. How sad it was to think that there was no such thing as a faithful mate. You mean to tell me, Eddie Murphy had told us right in his standup comedy film *Eddie Murphy Raw* way back when? Ms. Maybelle did have a point, though. I was quite miserable every time I thought about Bertrand's possible indiscretions and how much they just tore into my heart. I wanted to love him and work things out, but I just couldn't. It hurt too bad. It was too close to my past.

By the time I left Ms. Maybelle's house that evening, my mind was made up. I was going to leave Bertrand. And not because I hated him so much, but because I knew that I would never really trust him. I would never look at him the same; making love would never feel pure and honest. I'd never again feel like he really did love me. Eventually, we'd both be terribly miserable, and that wouldn't be fair to either of us. Especially to me, who had been faithful, even overlooking my own moral convictions.

Chapter 16

Dina

Everything Bertrand did was suspicious to me. Everything. If he showered for an extra five minutes, I'd peek in the tub to see if he was masturbating, with thoughts of Miranda on his mind for sure. If he was late coming in from work, I was unsettled with his explanation of trying to finish up a project or a meeting that ran over. If he dressed a particular kind of way, I wondered who he was on his way to meet. I shared my thoughts with Candis and Celeste when we met at Pizzeria Bianco that weekend, spliting one of the shop's specialties, the Wiseguy, a pizza made with roasted onion, smoked mozzarella and fennel Sausage.

"You messed up when you told him about those panties," Candis said. "Now you will never find out if he's cheating, because all he is going to do is hide it better."

She had a point. I'd alerted Bertrand that my antennae were up, so now he'd be super careful, whereas he might have gotten increasingly sloppy if I'd said nothing.

"You should have just kept it to yourself until you had more information," Candis added.

"That's easy to say when you don't have to sleep in the bed beside him," I argued. "After a while, saying that I have a headache while I try to figure things out doesn't really work."

"So don't say that. Just say no," Candis suggested.

"That sounds silly," Celeste commented. "How are you going to refuse to have sex with your man? She already thinks he's cheating. All that's going to do is push him further out there . . . if that's what he's doing."

"Well, I wouldn't keep sleeping with him if I thought he was slippin', tippin', and dippin'. That's how people mess around and catch stuff they can't get rid of," Candis argued.

Hearing her words made a knot form in my stomach, not that I hadn't thought about that before. It just seemed better to ignore the thought than embrace it.

"Seriously Dina, do you think he's cheating on you?" Celeste asked.

Before I could answer, Candis interjected, "You know what they say. If you think he's cheating, he's cheating. Don't you be no fool, Dina. You ain't crazy."

"She can't go around just being suspicious without cause, either."

"She's not being suspicious without cause. She's got a reason to be," Candis countered.

"Dina, have you talked to Bertrand about your insecurities?"

"We've had a couple of conversations, but they've not been pleasant," I mumbled.

"What is he saying?" Celeste asked.

"I bet he's saying what every man says when his woman asks him if he's cheating. 'No, baby! I love you, and I only want to make love to you! I'd be a fool to cheat on you.' Whatever. Call me Sunshine Anderson, because I've heard it all before," Candis said, ending in song.

"All right, Candis. Stop it. You're going to make me cry," I said, shoving her arm and almost knocking the slice of pizza she held out of her hand. "I just don't know what to believe. Which is the exact same place I was in years ago, when I was married to Cameron, and he was playing me like a damn video game."

"You're in a tough spot, Dina, but the only way to get past it is to talk with Bertrand," Celeste suggested. "You might have to get some counseling to deal with your unresolved issues with Cameron."

"Unresolved? Girl, please. I resolved those issues when I divorced him," I said in my defense.

"I don't think so. Sounds to me like you've carried the mistrust from your first marriage into your current relationship," Celeste almost whispered.

"No, I haven't! I've always trusted Bertrand up until now. I wasn't like this before, peeping and looking in every nook and corner for clues of something going on."

"I think you have and just don't realize it," Candis threw in. "Because why else would you be just randomly going through his drawers?"

"What's wrong with me doing that? We're an engaged couple. I could see if we were just dating and I was spending the night at his place, but I'm supposed to be his wife, and I have a right to look at everything in that house."

"You might have a right, but did you have a reason?" Celeste asked.

Which got me thinking. What had been my reason for digging through his things? "I don't believe in living life blind. I think everybody ought to keep their eyes open, and there's nothing wrong with being aware of your surroundings."

"Being aware of your surroundings and looking for dirt are two different things." Celeste concentrated her eyes on me with raised brows.

"I say more power to you. If there is dirt to be found, find it before it attacks and kills you. You've heard about people getting sick because their house is full of mold and they didn't know it. An ounce of prevention is better than a pound of cure," Candis said, rolling her eyes.

"Finding dirt is not prevention, Candis," Celeste said. "Finding dirt means the damage is done, and that's the part Dina doesn't know yet."

And it was the not knowing that was killing me. It worried me all that night and throughout the next day, while I was at work.

Bertrand was in the driveway, washing his car, when I got home from work, and I found it hard to look at him. My mind was completely consumed with his possible infidelity. All I could think about was the panties I found, who they belonged to, and why they'd been in his possession.

"Hey, babe," he called, playfully flicking the water hose my way, but he knew better than to wet my hair.

"Hey."

Bertrand dropped the hose and came over to peck me on the lips, which I allowed, but it felt all wrong.

"How was work?" he asked.

"Long, as usual. Let me get changed." After digging in folks' hair all day, the first thing I always wanted to do once I got home was scrub their germs and bits of hair off of me.

While I was in the shower, I thought through how my next conversation with Bertrand should go. I had to confront him, or else it was going to eat me up inside. I could already feel heartbreak settling in, even though I wanted to give him the benefit of the doubt. As I scrubbed my body, I took an assessment of my size and figure. My weight was up ten pounds. Suddenly, I felt ugly and unattractive, and I couldn't help but wonder if Bertrand still found me as attractive as he had a year ago, when he asked me to be his wife. I'd said yes, but Lord knows, I wished I had said no.

Compared to Equanto, Bertrand wasn't a bad mate. As a matter of fact, Equanto made Bertrand look like a superstar. He loved me, or so I wanted to believe, was an excellent provider, paid the bills on time, and enjoyed spoiling me. He was always bringing me flowers and trinkets and doing all kinds of stuff that women loved. At least that was how it began. It was never until after you moved in with a person or said "I do" that you found out who you were really dealing with, and like I said, I wished I had declined his proposal. Now I knew him to be insecure and controlling, and he treated me like a child.

I still remembered the time I pissed him off real good about a month after moving into his house by making an "unapproved" purchase. I had gotten a good paycheck at work and had been eyeing one of those little book reading devices for months. On payday, I stopped by the bookstore, looked at the few different models they had to offer, and picked out a color device and a nice cover for it. The cover was ridiculously priced. But if I was gonna splurge, I was gonna splurge!

I came in the house about an hour later than usual, swinging my bag with my purchase, to find Bertrand silently fuming in the kitchen, where he was popping a few hot dogs in the microwave.

"Hey, honey," I greeted, as happy as a jaybird.

Bertrand barely cracked his lips to utter a response.

"What's wrong with you?"

"Where have you been?" he grumbled.

"I stopped by the store to get this!" Excited, I swung the bag up and thrust it toward him. "I got one of those book things!" Digging in the bag for my new toy, I didn't notice right away the disapproving glare Bertrand wore on his face. "It's the color one," I chimed, carefully handling my device like it was a newborn baby. "Whenever I want to buy a book, I can just tap on the screen and it will download onto here."

"How much did that cost?" he grunted, taking his quick meal out of the microwave.

I quoted the price and explained that I'd used my extra money to treat myself.

"So you're just out there spending money without letting me know about it?" he said, folding his arms across his chest.

"What do you mean? I'm telling you now."

"You're telling me after the fact. Don't you think you should have talked to me about this before you just went out and bought something?"

Really I didn't, but I gave it a moment of thought. "What's the big deal, babe?"

"We're engaged to be married, Dina, or did you forget that?"

"Of course I didn't forget, but I'm saying . . ." I paused for half a second to throw on a puzzled face. "I can't buy anything without talking to you first?"

"Why would you think that was okay?" he questioned, squirting ketchup on his food.

"Well, first of all, because I'm grown, and secondly, I didn't realize I needed *your* permission to spend *my* money."

"So you can just do whatever you want to do, then, huh?"

This was ridiculous to me, but clearly, it was a problem for Bertrand.

"And then you didn't even call me to let me know you weren't coming straight home," he added.

"Babe," I sighed, "I stopped at the store." My bit of excitement about having a new toy was diminished.

"So you couldn't call first?"

"Yes, I could have, but I'm here now, and you can see where I've been."

"You're acting like you still want to be single, Dina," he said, carrying his plate to the den, where he had been watching ESPN. "Now I'm sitting here, having to eat hot dogs and chips for dinner."

"No, I'm acting like I'm a grown woman," I shot back, following him into the den. "And if you had just been patient, you wouldn't be eating a carnival meal right now."

He didn't respond, other than rolling his eyes at me.

"So I can't stop at the store, and I can't spend any money without talking to you first?" I asked, feeling that the conversation was unfinished and the issue was certainly unresolved. By now my hands were on my hips, and my temperature was on low boil.

"Tell me what marriage means to you," he said.

"It doesn't mean that I gotta get your permission for everything I do," I snapped.

"Maybe I'm confused, then, about what marriage is supposed to be. I'm sitting here waiting for you to get home so you can fix some dinner and we can enjoy a nice evening together, and then not only do you not call, and I don't have a clue where you are, but on top of that, you're out spending money." He shook his head, as if he were grossly disappointed.

I was annoyed by his thinking. "It's not like I stopped for drinks," I countered. "And it's not like I spent bill money."

"Okay, so the deal is we can stop wherever we want on the way home from work without saying a word to each other unless we're stopping for drinks." He paused to let that thought sink in for a minute. "And as long as it's not the bill money that's being spent, the sky's the limit on spending. We can just go buy whatever we want when we want, regardless of the cost."

When Bertrand put it like that, I could see where he was coming from just a little bit. Only a little, though, because we weren't even talking about a hundred dollars here. At the same time, I knew how Bertrand thought. He would take things to the extreme and was liable to come home tomorrow with a new car without mentioning it to me first. Not that he had to. I didn't know whether to offer a light apology or stand my ground, but the whole thing was stupid to me.

"No, I'm not saying that at all, but I am tired of talking about it, because I feel like I deserved to treat myself to something nice. I had the money to do it, and I don't feel like I need your permission or approval to enjoy my life. I ain't no kid, and you ain't my daddy." I turned around, grabbed the bag with my book thingy, the cover, the packaging, and the papers, then commented over my shoulder, "I'm going to get in the tub and enjoy a good book."

Sitting in the tub with a new read, I could hardly enjoy myself, thinking about the conversation we'd just had. Again, I could understand not making major purchases without there being some type of discussion, but not over this petty thing. This wasn't what I would consider a major purchase. Bertrand spent money on stuff all the time, as a matter of fact. Recently I'd seen a couple of bags from the sporting goods store, new golf balls, and some computer software, come to think of it. There was no discussion between us for those purchases. But *I* was supposed to run to him and get permission when I wanted to buy something? I didn't think so.

Once I'd gotten out of the tub, I lotioned and perfumed my body, put on something sexy, and brushed my hair up into a sexy, wispy updo, so that Bertrand and I could make up by making love and going to sleep holding each other, like we always did. Sex always made men forget the stupid stuff.

Feeling renewed and sexy, and with our earlier conversation-slash-argument more than an hour behind us, I waltzed downstairs, ready to seduce my man. Before I went in the den, I padded to the kitchen to pour a couple glasses of wine.

Bertrand was still reclined on the sofa, where I'd seen him last, his empty plate on the floor beside him.

"Got room for me?" I asked in my sultry sex kitten voice. The teddy I had on had my cheeks poking out the back, so I casually turned to let him see, then turned back to face him.

"You can sit over there. I'm comfortable," he said, cutting his eye to an alternate chair.

After a second of hesitation, I tried again. "You can't just scoot over a little bit?" I offered him a glass, expecting him to take it and make room.

He pushed a sigh from his mouth as he reached for the glass. "Let me enjoy the game, Dina, okay?"

Was he serious? I stood for a few seconds, wondering what the hell was going on, but then retreated back down the hallway to the bedroom. Sitting on the edge of the bed, I had three different emotions going on at once. Firstly, I was confused as to why Bertrand was having such a crazy reaction to something that was really nothing. Secondly, I was hurt. He'd rejected me. Not rejected me in a pair of sweats and a raggedy

T-shirt, but he'd rejected me in some lingerie. With my booty hanging out and all. Then, finally, I was angry, because I felt like he was being unreasonable and controlling. So what if I bought myself something? We weren't getting put out of the house because of it. I sulked for maybe ten minutes before I semi-shrugged it off and grabbed my e-reader again. I'd been seeing statuses all over Facebook about people curling up with a glass of wine and their varied devices. It hadn't been my plan to try out that specific relaxation method, but I figured I might as well make the most of the moment.

I plopped down on the chaise in the corner of my bedroom, curling my feet beneath me, and got lost in a Zora Neale Hurston story. Before I knew it, her words and that wine rocked me to sleep. When I woke up a couple hours later, Bertrand had already gotten into bed, without bothering to wake me up. That was unlike him, especially because of the way I was dressed. If it were up to him, we'd have sex two and three times a day, every day, except the day when my period was at its absolute heaviest. So for him to be in bed without trying to get himself some was definitely out of the norm.

I stood, stretched, brushed my teeth, then crawled in bed and nestled up to Bertrand's back. I wasn't feeling particularly horny, but I had to get over this rejection I felt by offering myself to him again and having him accept. I wrapped my arms around him, then let a hand slide down to fondle his manhood. He placed his hand on mine, lifted it up, and moved it behind him.

"Stop, Dina," he uttered, but I persisted, sliding my hand back across his hip and to his front. "I said stop," he said more adamantly, and this time he tossed my hand away.

"What's wrong with you?" I asked, sucking my teeth.

"I'm ready to ask you that same thing," he said, slightly looking over his shoulder toward me, but our eyes hardly connected.

"What do you mean, Bertrand?"

"You know damn well what I mean. All of a sudden you want to act like my wife, but a few hours ago, you must have been like, 'To hell with my husband and our marriage. I'ma do what I damn well please.'"

"We're not even married yet, and it wasn't even like that. Believe me, I had no idea that me spending a few dollars was going to turn into a silly fight, else I would have called you first."

"Oh, so this is silly to you?"

"The way you're acting is silly, yes," I declared. "I mean, what is really going on that you are this bent out of shape over an hour's worth of time and a less than one-hundred-dollar purchase?"

"When you figure it out, you let me know." He pulled the covers toward him and dropped his head on his pillow. "Until then I'm done."

We didn't speak for about three days after that. I wondered if that was when he tiptoed out of the house to be with someone else.

Chapter 17

Candis

Since SeanMichael's phone had been cut off, I couldn't wait to get home every day to get on Facebook to read his in-box messages. Luckily, he had Internet access at his job, so we were able to stay in contact.

The first thing I did when I got in was turn on my computer and log in, then warm up a quick Lean Cuisine meal. This extra weight was killing me, and I was determined to get rid of it before SeanMichael and I met, whenever that would be. Since I'd eaten poorly all day—doughnuts for breakfast and McDonald's for lunch—I thought the least I could do was attempt to eat right at dinnertime.

As expected, I did have an in-box message waiting for me. *Yes!*

> SeanMichael Monroe
> Hi Beautiful!
> I miss hearing your voice, but I'm so blessed to be able to see your smiling face right here on your profile. I hope you are having a great day.
> SM
>
> Candis I'mTheOne Turner
> Hey SeanMichael,
> My day was long and boring since I didn't get a

chance to talk to you. You always make my day brighter, and it seems to go by a lot smoother and faster when I can hear your voice. How long do you think it will be before you're able to get your phone back on?

I told my friends about you this week, and of course, they are riding my case. I don't even care, though, because they are in some pretty jacked-up relationships and don't have room to talk about anybody.

Dina is marrying a man who only wants a trophy or a puppet. She can barely leave her house without him almost stalking her to find out what she is doing and who she's with. I can't believe she's still engaged. They look like they got it going on, but he's screwing around on her. She can't prove it, but that is what she believes, and I can't blame her. She found some panties in her house that didn't belong to her and a few text messages. He is playing dumb, but he ain't fooling nobody.

And Celeste just lets her man treats her any kind of way. Lie, cheat, steal . . . only thing left is kill. It's really sad, and I feel sorry for her, but you can't make someone get up if they like being a doormat. Like I said, neither one of them has room to talk. That's not stopping them from talking, though.

SeanMichael Monroe
Babe,
We already know people are always going to have something to say. People have been talking about me my whole life, and the times that I let their talk influence me are some of the times that I have the biggest regrets. What I've found out is God gave my life to me. Not to my momma, my

daddy, my family, or my friends. He gave me my own mind, my own will, and my own emotions, and only I can give other people the power to control them. But guess what? I choose not to do that. I choose to keep my own power. I don't care what anyone says, and who says it. I love you, and I can't wait to make you my wife.

Candis I'mThe One Turner
Your wife? Wow, SeanMichael! I wasn't expecting you to say that.

SeanMichael Monroe
I know, but it's true. Even from a distance, you make my life complete. You're the best part of my day, and you are my destiny.

Candis I'mTheOne Turner
How do you know that?

SeanMichael Monroe
Because I prayed and asked God to show me a woman who loves Him and who could love me and whom I could love, and the next thing I knew, we were talking. I am not one to look a gift horse in the mouth. I know what I prayed for, and I thank God every day that He brought you into my life.

Candis I'mTheOne Turner
Wow! You really make me smile. Did you know that?

SeanMichael Monroe
I'm glad I could do that, and if you give me the chance, I want to make you smile every single day of the rest of your life as your man.

Candis I'mTheOne Turner
Well, I don't know if I am ready for marraige, especially since we've never met in person, but it's nice to know that you are always thinking about me.

SeanMichael Monroe
I do more than think about you, Candis. I dream about you, I pray for you, I respect you, and I love you.

Candis I'mTheOne Turner
You better stop it, or you're going to make me fall in love with you.

SeanMichael Monroe
And I would be so honored if you would.

Candis I'mTheOne Turner
If you keep it up, it would only be a matter of time.

SeanMichael Monroe
I ain't got nothing but time, and I will wait as long as it takes.

We sent messages back and forth for another two hours, talking about some of everything. He was such a nice guy, at least online. He was forever posting nice little sentiments, lines of poetry, romantic videos, and pictures of flowers on my wall to let me know that I'd crossed his mind throughout his day.

And to kill that noise about him posting fake pictures of what he looked like, we had begun talking live over Skype, so I was able to verify what he looked like at various times of the day. I'd seen him with his sleepy morning face on, I'd seen him at the end of his workday, and I'd seen him right before bedtime. His lips were thick and luscious, begging to cover my own when he talked. His five o'clock shadow gave his face character and sex appeal, and I always saw a smile in his eyes, even when he complained about being exhausted from work. A few times he'd hit me up with his shirt off, and the pecs on that man were nothing short of delicious looking. He looked like he could bench-press three hundred pounds without breaking a sweat. He was eye candy for sure.

He'd taken me on a virtual tour of his house, carrying around a Web camera and posting videos. It looked like a typical bachelor's pad. From what I could see, things were simplistic, a little grimy, outdated, and in a bit of a disarray, just like you'd expect from a bachelor. The pictures he had hanging on the walls didn't complement each other and looked randomly placed, as did his overall home decor. Everything looked mismatched and pieced together. I saw nothing that made me think that a woman lived there with him. His place could really use a woman's touch.

Finally, I logged off, got in the shower and then in bed. I felt silly about letting my imagination run away with me, thinking, What if SeanMichael and I did end up together? Even as I slept, I thought about how it would be to be Mrs. SeanMichael Monroe.

Chapter 18

Dina

We'd not argued about my suspicions in nearly two months, but the tension in the house was apparent. Bertrand and I had been tiptoeing around each other, as if we were invisible to one another. I remembered how we used to kiss every morning and lay in bed for an extra two minutes or more, just holding each other, not wanting to pull away. Now he slept on his side of the bed, and I slept on mine, with enough room between us for Santa Claus to sleep comfortably. Our mornings started with silence, and our movements were careful and calculated so that we wouldn't end up too close to each other at any given time. It was painfully sad, but I didn't know what to do to make it go away.

There were some parts of my heart that wanted so badly to be loved by Bertrand again, but it all felt like a lie now. All that I'd believed him to be—honest, faithful, a man of integrity— had been washed away. Now I didn't know who I was looking at. I just couldn't act like those feelings and that pain didn't exist. Bertrand did try a little to kiss me, but I found myself turning away, not able to block images of him kissing another woman on the mouth, on her breasts, and below her navel. I wanted to enjoy him sexually, but I couldn't get past him sliding in and out of another woman's body, then turning around and experiencing that same pleasure with me. As great a sex life as we had, with Bertrand satisfying me completely almost every time, it just wasn't pleasurable anymore.

I remembered how he would often whisper, "I love you, Dina" while we were making love, and even afterward, when I lay in his arms, still overcome with ecstasy that had me shuddering and stuttering. "I love you," he would say, and I believed that fool! It sounded so right, and it felt so good. Not just physically, but emotionally, it was divine. And then to think that all that he'd shared with me so passionately, he was giving away to other women too? I wouldn't go so far as to say I hated my fiancé, but I couldn't embrace him in the same way that I once had.

I prepared dinner with special thought tonight, because I needed to set a tone and atmosphere of calmness and peace, even if what I had to say wouldn't be the most peaceful thing he'd heard. The meal was simple, just some grilled chicken with mixed vegetables, some freshly baked bread, and some wine. This would be nice if the conversation were to be romantic. I just didn't want Bertrand to think I was acting out of anger.

He came in the door and looked surprised to have the aroma of a cooked meal hit his nostrils. It had been a while since I'd cared enough to cook a meal.

"Hey," he mumbled.

"Hi." I continued scuffling around the kitchen. "How was work?"

He shrugged. "It was okay."

"I cooked dinner," I announced.

"I see. What brought that on?"

"Thought we should sit down to dinner and talk."

"Okay," he said suspiciously.

"The food will be ready in about ten minutes or so."

"All right. I'm going to go wash my hands and face, then."

He disappeared down the hallway and into our bedroom. By the time he came back, the food had been on the table for fifteen minutes and had to be reheated in the microwave. The first few minutes of the meal were silent as I stared between his face and my plate.

"So what did you want to talk about?" he finally asked.

"Bertrand," I began, then paused, as if I hadn't rehearsed the words in my mind and even with my mouth several times over the past couple of weeks. "Babe, I can't do this anymore. I just can't."

He looked at me, chewing his food methodically but not commenting, then turned his eyes back to his plate.

"I've tried to forget everything that's happened and to go back to being how we were, but I can't do it. It's too painful, and I can barely look at you anymore."

Bertrand nodded as he set his fork on the plate.

"I know that I really need to walk away from the situation, instead of growing more and more bitter every day, and I don't feel like I can embrace you or love you given how I'm feeling right now."

"I love you, Dina. We're supposed to promise to be together for better or for worse," he stated calmly.

"But we're also supposed to be ready to forsake all others and give ourselves to each other only. You violated that. You broke our pending covenant when you did that, Bertrand."

He nodded again, but I couldn't tell if it was in agreement or simply in acknowledgment.

"And I don't feel like I can become your wife and treat you like a wife should treat her husband with that rolling around in the back of my mind nearly every second of every day. Every time I lay beside you, every time I want to make love to you, every time I want to miss you, it's in the way, and I can't move beyond it."

"You can't, or you don't want to?"

I paused to think about what he'd said before I got offended. "Maybe I don't want to. It's not fair to me to force me to share myself with you after you've damaged the relationship and me. It's not fair to expect me to just accept your trash and swallow it, then say it was delicious and ask you for some more."

Bertrand stared at me.

"You made a fool of me, Bertrand. You took advantage of my trust and made a fool of me. I can't live another day like this."

"I understand. I effed up. I really did." He rose to his feet, leaving more than half his meal on his plate. "All I can say to you at this point is, I'm sorry, Dina. I'm sorry for hurting you. I'm sorry for breaking your heart and for cheating on you. I'm sorry for making you feel like you can't trust me. If I could take it all back, I would. There's no way in the world I would be the same fool twice." He shook his head, looking across the room and out the kitchen window. "I'm sorry, babe."

He walked out of the kitchen and into the den, where he switched on the TV.

Now that I'd said all that, what was I going to do? Business at the shop had picked up some, but not enough for me to be able to move out and back into my own place. Nothing had really changed with my finances. Sure, Bertrand paid the bills, but they were all his bills. He'd not taken on mine, like I thought he would. I did get caught up on my bills, but it would be too easy to get behind again if I moved out. Even so, I'd already had the conversation, so now I was going to have to figure out my next step.

Chapter 19

Celeste

After clocking out, I headed to my car to get my purse out of the trunk so I could pick up a few items to make dinner with. I hated that there were no lockers in the store for employees to keep their personal items. If it didn't fit in the pockets of the smocks cashiers wore, it was at risk of being taken or riffled through. I'd learned the hard way that I couldn't leave my purse around Equanto, especially if there was money in it. That would be like throwing money straight out the window on a windy day.

My heart dropped down in my shoes when I looked across the lot and saw that the trunk of my car was open. Fully. My breathing increased as I began to panic, already knowing what I would find—that my purse was gone. My tears were instant as I searched the contents of the trunk, wanting my purse to magically appear. I hadn't buried it under anything, although there was a basket of laundry that had not yet made it to the Laundromat, a box of clothes and shoes that the boys had outgrown, which I'd been meaning to drop off at Goodwill, a spare tire, and other random items. Everything in the trunk looked to be untouched and in its normal disarray, except my purse was gone. Quickly I shuffled stuff around, but to no avail.

It was bad enough that there was about two hundred dollars in my purse, but it also contained my driver's license, my and the kids' Social Security cards, our birth certificates, their shot records, and every other document that was important to me and proved my existence here on earth. They were now gone from my possession.

"Lord Jesus!" I screamed into the air, smearing tears into my face, walking in a small circle, shooting my eyes back into the trunk every few seconds to make sure I hadn't just overlooked my purse. Finally accepting the reality that I'd been jacked, I pulled my cell from my pocket and called the police, and while I waited for them to arrive, I called Equanto. Thankfully, I'd broken the rules by having my cell phone on my person during work hours, which was grounds for being written up.

"Somebody stole my purse," I sobbed into the phone.

"Whatchu mean?"

"I came out the store, and somebody had picked the lock on the trunk and took my purse."

"See? When stuff like that happens to me, you be thinking I'm making it up. Now you see what I'm talking about." There was no compassion or sympathy in his voice, which angered me.

"I don't want to hear that right now, E," I yelled into the phone. "They took my whole purse. Not just my money, but all my IDs and stuff."

"Where was you at? You probably went somewhere you ain't had no business."

"I've been at work all day," I shrieked. "I'll call you back. The police are here."

I talked to the officers for about thirty minutes, completing a report and watching them circle the car and scan the lot like they were looking for clues, but they ultimately told me it wasn't likely that anything would be recovered. Not bothering to call E back, I drove home in a cloud of depression, knowing that I was going to have to make some deals with the bill collectors and cross my fingers in hopes that the rental office lady would show me some mercy once I showed her the police report. There was no way I'd be able to pay my rent on time now. Then I still had to replace all our documents and whatnot. I prayed that by the time I got home, Equanto would have somewhere to go. I wasn't up for dealing with his mess tonight.

As soon as I pulled into the parking lot, he came rushing out of the house, ready to jump in the car and go somewhere. I wanted him to leave, but not with the car. He walked up to the driver's side and opened the door.

"Get out. I need to go somewhere," he said, thrusting his hand forward for the keys.

"You can't use the car," I replied without hesitation, turning off the ignition.

"Why not?" he demanded.

"Because the police have to come and do the fingerprints on the back," I said, making it up off the top of my head. They had told me in the store parking lot that it didn't look like they could get a clean print from the car, because the lock had been picked with a tool, so it hadn't been handled enough, but Equanto didn't know that. His face froze like I had just tazed him, and at that point, I knew he was guilty.

"They was s'posed to do that when they first came," he said, far less aggressively than he'd ordered me to get out of the car.

"They didn't have the stuff with them, and I told them that I needed to get home to the kids, or else they were gonna be locked out the house, so they are supposed to meet me here in a few minutes."

His eyes darted nervously to the entrance of the apartment complex. "A'ight. I'll just catch the bus, then."

I'd never seen Equanto back down and leave the house so fast, scared his ass was about to get locked up.

I sat in the car for another twenty minutes, completely immobilized, but I knew I couldn't sit there forever, since the boys were in the house by themselves. The rest of the night was stressful, to say the least. I tried not to let my boys know when I was incredibly upset, but this time I couldn't help it. When I came in the door, they rushed me, with their voices rattling off a series of complaints, from "Ma, we hungry" to "Can you check my homework?" to "Daddy said to tell you to wash our clothes, 'cause he didn't have time to do it."

"Stop!" I said before they got too far into their roll. "Stop for a minute and listen to me." As if I had hit a button on a remote control, the boys stopped their blubbering and looked at me attentively. "I need some time to myself tonight. Okay?"

"Yes, ma'am," they answered in unison. They addressed me as "ma'am" only when they were in trouble or when they knew, beyond a shadow of a doubt, I was dead serious.

"Y'all know I love you, but right now I don't want to answer no questions, I don't want to check homework, and I don't want to wash clothes, play video games, listen to you read, watch you do a dance, or hear y'all fighting." I paused and concentrated my focus on each one of them, one at a time. "I have a really bad headache, and all I want right now is some peace and quiet, okay?"

"Yes, ma'am."

"Now, Linwood, you're the oldest. What I need you to do is fix you and your brothers a ham and cheese sandwich, some chips, and a banana and pour y'all some juice. Make sure you use the paper plates, because I'm not washing dishes tonight. When y'all finish, put the plates in the trash and the cups in the sink. Then y'all can watch Nickelodeon until bedtime."

"Yes, ma'am," they again responded collectively.

"I'm going in my room, and I do not want to be bothered unless a stranger breaks the door down, the house is on fire, or one of you is bleeding. Understand?"

"Yes, ma'am."

"And I'm leaving the door open to make sure y'all keep quiet," I added, walking down the hall and to my bedroom. If I closed the door, they would start off being quiet but would eventually reach a noise level that sounded like a full-blown house party. I still ran that risk, but if I kept my bedroom door open, they'd be less likely to escalate.

What I wanted to do was go in the closet and start ripping Equanto's stuff from the hangers, then have a *Waiting to Exhale,* burn-his-stuff-up moment. But I didn't need to waste any energy on anything that wasn't going to result in some level of resolution. It sure as hell would have made me feel better, though. Instead, I sat on the bed and prayed for a few minutes that God would help me get all my stuff back as quickly as possible, that He would move on the heart of the rent lady, and that He would calm my spirit down enough so that I wouldn't kill my husband the next time I saw him.

Equanto wasn't back by the time I left for work the next day, probably because I still needed time to cool down. The boys could tell that there was still tension in the air from the previous night, and acted accordingly, getting themselves ready for school. After seeing them off, I stopped by the rental office to do my begging, but there were too many people there for me to get a private moment. I'd have to come back later. As I drove myself to work, I prayed that God would give me the grace to make it through my day. I pushed my keys and cell in my smock pocket and dragged myself inside the store.

"How are you doing this morning?" Some dude was sitting in the break room, dragging his finger around on an iPad, when I walked in to clock in for the day.

"Fine," I answered without thought and not bothering to look up. I pushed my time card into the machine until I heard it stamp, stuck it back in the rack on the wall, then poured myself a cup of coffee to go with the doughnut sticks I had shoved in my smock pocket.

"How long is your shift today?"

Why was this man talking to me? "I get off at two," I snapped unintentionally, too mentally distracted to pay him much mind.

"That's not too bad," he commented.

I didn't respond, but stood silently, stirring sugar and powdered creamer into my paper cup.

"Are you all right? You seem like you're carrying the weight of the world on your shoulders."

This time I did look up at him as I pushed a sigh through my nostrils. I saw sincerity in his eyes as he looked at me through a pair of black framed glasses. I had seen him around the store, mostly in the produce section, but had never been in close enough proximity to actually attempt a conversation.

"I'm sorry. I got a lot on my mind this morning that's kinda got me in a bad mood, but that has nothing to do with you, and you don't deserve that."

"It's all right. Life happens to us all, but we always live through it, right?"

"I guess we do," I answered with a little chuckle.

"And one thing I've learned, no matter how bad things are, they could always be worse."

That's because he didn't have to deal with a jackass of a spouse every day like I did. Well . . . I couldn't say that, because I didn't rightfully know if he did or not. Maybe he did, but I wouldn't bet any money on it, since his ring finger was bare.

"You're right." I nodded with a half grin. "Let me start over. Good morning. I'm Celeste. I have to give you an elbow bump because I've been sneezing in my hand and don't want to get you sick." I leaned my right elbow toward him, instead of sticking my hand out for the standard handshake.

Appreciating my consideration, he laughed and reciprocated the gesture. "Nice to meet you, Celeste. I'm Keith."

"Likewise."

Not meaning to, I released as much air as a fully inflated balloon that had been pricked with a straight pin when I took a seat, letting out a "Whew!" I caught myself by surprise, and a wave of embarrassment washed over me.

Keith acted like he didn't notice, but he had to, because I knew I just about blew him out of his chair. Almost immediately, he stood, slid his device into a sleeve, tucked it under his arm, and said, "Well, I hope your day gets better."

"Thanks." I blushed. Suddenly I was ashamed of the cakey treat I'd pulled out of my pocket and sat on the table just before I sat down. How hard would it have been for me to have grabbed a banana or an orange or something? Replaying the events from the day before made me dismiss that thought and fall into my familiar pattern of being comforted by my taste buds. "I'll start tomorrow," I promised myself . . . like I'd done a hundred times before.

I used to look forward to going to work just to get away from Equanto, but Keith's morning company soon became my motivation for leaving my house every morning. He always engaged in pleasant conversation and even had a compliment or two for me. Sometimes I got to work a whole hour before my shift just to talk to him. On those days, I'd eat my sweets before he got there, then enjoy a piece of fruit once he arrived. Caring what he thought of me, I didn't want him to see me eating unhealthy snacks. I'd started putting on a little makeup again, which I hadn't done since I left my old job, and sometimes I caught myself trying to suck my stomach in. I had to laugh at myself, because there wasn't enough sucking in in the world to make a difference with all the belly I had beneath my smock. I did it anyway, though, feeling like I was on a little date every morning.

It was during these little dates that I told Keith about my three boys and my husband and a few other details from my crazy, mixed-up life. He told me he had a teenage daughter, whom he rarely saw because she lived out of state.

"I can't imagine life without my kids," I said.

"It's tough," he said with a nod. "Real tough." With a few passes of his finger on the screen of his tablet, he showed me a picture of a cheery-looking girl with braces. "This is my heart right here."

"She's gorgeous," I commented, taking the tablet in my hand and swiping through some other photos. "What's her name?"

"Jordan. She's the love of my life."

"That's nice." I couldn't help but smile. I loved to hear men talk about how much they loved their kids. "Maybe I'll get to meet her one day."

"Yep. Definitely."

I liked the sound of that. It sounded like he hoped we'd be friends for a while. I wasn't about to forsake my marriage vows, but it felt nice having some positive male attention in my life. There was nothing wrong with have a good male friend around, just to make me feel like a woman, since my husband wasn't going to do it.

Chapter 20

Celeste

"So you want me to cosign on you stepping out on your husband?" was Candis's response when I asked her if I could invite Keith to her birthday party as she drove me home from work, since Equanto claimed he needed the car to go to a job interview. I figured her party would be a great place to for us to interact outside of work. It would be a mixed crowd, we could arrive separately, and onlookers wouldn't necessarily put us together. It was the best I could do without feeling like I was out on a date with a man other than my husband.

"I'm not stepping out on E, Candis. Keith is just a friend. That's it."

"What kind of friend? One with benefits?" she challenged with raised brows.

"Girl, no! You know I'm married."

"Yes, I do know. So why are you trying to be all in this man's face?"

"Would you rather me bring Equanto with me?" She knew he was a straight-up hell-raiser.

Immediately her expression changed, and she couldn't help but laugh. "You got a good point! What's his number? I'll invite him myself."

While Dina, Candis, and I decorated the community clubhouse in Candis' neighborhood, I was all giddy inside about seeing Keith. He was all I could think about while the three of us embellished the clubhouse with pink and black diva-themed decorations. From the stereo Anthony Hamilton's voice filled the room, giving us something to work to, and when he crooned the lyrics to "The Point of It All," I imagined someone, specifically Keith, serenading me and meaning those words. Not just saying them out of obligation.

I started daydreaming, envisioning myself in his arms, leaning back against his chest, standing on the shore of a beach somewhere, just enjoying the waves washing over our feet, with his arms wrapped around my shoulders. We had on jeans that were rolled up at the ankle and crisp white shirts that dropped over our waistlines instead of being tucked into our pants. Then we held hands as we strolled, laughing and talking and stopping every few steps to pick up a shell.

Unknowingly, a smile crept across my face as I imagined what it would be like to be in love and have someone love me back.

"What are you grinning about?" Dina asked as she passed by me, suddenly making me aware of my silly thoughts and expression.

"Just thinking about something one of the boys told me about school the other day," I lied.

"It must have been mighty funny for you to be cheesing like that." She grabbed a folded tablecloth for the gift table and disappeared into the next room, freeing me from making up some story to explain my unintentional smile.

I watched the door like a hawk, waiting for Keith to arrive, and when he did, I tried to look happily occupied with chatting with other guests, but I saw him scan the room in search of me. It took only a few minutes for him to casually make his way over to where I was.

"Hey, Celeste," he greeted with a smile.

"Keith!" I beamed, as if his presence surprised me. "Glad you were able to make it. It's good to see you."

"It's good to be seen, but even better to see you." He bent down and kissed my cheek and embraced me with a quick hug. "You look amazing."

"Thanks." From the way I blushed, anybody would have thought he'd laid me down and given it to me real good. I cleared my throat and had a knee-jerk action. "Let me go get you something to eat."

Turning my back to him and heading for the food table, I felt my cheeks rise in a grin. I was super happy to see Keith. I piled food onto a plate, then stopped at the drink station, where Dina stood ladling punch into cups.

"He's here!" I semi-whispered.

"Where?"

"Over there, near the DJ table. He has on all black." I dared not turn around but watched Dina's eyes casually search the room to catch a glimpse of him.

"Girl, he's cute! You better hope your husband don't come busting in here."

"We're just friends. Nothing more than that." That was the truth, even though I would have loved for it to have been more.

"Yeah. That's what Candis used to say about SeanMichael, and now he's her boyfriend and she's never even seen him."

"That's a mess," I stated. "He should have at least come to her birthday party, but I'm glad he didn't, because I did text Russell and tell him to come."

"You did what?" Dina gasped.

"What? It's the only thing I could think of to get her mind off of Mr. East Coast. You know she don't need to be dating him."

"She's gonna kill you if she finds out you invited him."

"Well, she's not going to find out, and even if she did, she can't prove it."

"How do you know he is not going to show up with his new woman and make matters worse?"

"Because I told him not to. Duh!" I said, grabbing a drink from her hand. "Oh, snap! There he is too!"

Chapter 21

Candis

"Happy birthday, beautiful," I heard a voice say to me from behind.

"Thank you!" I answered before turning around and finding myself standing face-to-face with Russell. Who invited him? I sure didn't, and I didn't know whether to smile politely, cry, or slap him in his face. Before I chose one of the three, he extended his arms for a hug, and I cordially obliged. As soon as our bodies came together in an embrace, which lasted all of three seconds, I was caught up. The feeling of his chest against mine was comfortable, alluring, and sexy. Instantly, I remembered him intimately and craved him. I had to catch my breath and pull away.

"What are you doing here?" I smiled out of both sincerity and confusion.

"Your birthday was set up as a reminder on my phone. I heard you were having a little get-together," he said and glanced quickly around the room. "And I couldn't just let the day pass without acknowledging it."

"Did you bring your fiancée?" My eyes darted around his body, then around the room. I didn't really expect him to have anyone with him.

He dropped his head in a chuckle, then looked up again. "No."

"Does she know you're here?" With a slight swivel of my hand, my wine swirled around in my diva glass.

"I guess you could say that," Russell said with a slow head nod.

"What do you mean?" As I was speaking, I remembered how sexy I looked in the stretchy black minidress I wore. I poked my chest out a little bit and casually placed my hand on my hip. "You only told her as much as you wanted her to know."

He hesitated for a few seconds, then said, "She knows you and I are still friends." I rolled my eyes at the word *friends*. "And she knows that I was dropping by a friend's party."

"Uninvited," I added, but that time my smile was cynical, as I remembered the parts of our involvement that I didn't like so much. And the fact that he was someone else's man now.

"Oh, is it like that?"

"I don't remember inviting you." I shook my head quickly with a shrug. "Did you at least bring a gift? Oh yeah, I forgot. You don't do gifts." Russell hadn't given me so much as an Easter egg, and it reminded me of one of the many reasons why I'd dismissed him from my life.

"I didn't realize a gift was required."

Same old Russell.

I shook my head and started to walk off. He was getting my emotions stirred up, and not in a good way.

"Wait a minute, Candis," he said, reaching out to grab my arm.

"Look. It's my birthday, and I want to enjoy it, unlike last year, when I waited all evening for you to come pick me up to take me out and you never showed. Do you remember that?"

"I'm sorry," he said, twisting his lips.

"And now you are about to get married, and you show up here like you can just walk in and out of my life whenever you get good and ready, and I'm supposed to be just overjoyed about that, right? I mean, I'm supposed to be that desperate that I will settle for someone else's man because he comes crashing in on my birthday party and didn't even bring a damn gift." It took everything within me to keep my composure and not let my body language communicate to the entire room the anger I felt. "If you really want me to have a happy birthday, Russell"—I paused and put on my sweetest smile—"get the hell out of here."

Russell and all his fine-ness stared back at me, as if my words had made him a statue. The only thing that moved was his eyes, which studied mine for a hint of weakness. I didn't show an ounce.

"There's the door." I nodded.

Shaking his head in what I assumed was defeat, he turned away and headed toward the exit, while I turned and headed for the bathroom, needing to pull myself together real quick. Leaning back against the sink, I cupped my hands around my mouth and nose and inhaled. I could still smell his signature cologne lingering on my skin from when he hugged me. Lord knows that man was looking and smelling some kinda good, and I wanted him some kinda bad. Even if it was just for old times' sake or for closure, or just because I hadn't had a good piece of ding-a-ling since he and I broke up. I mean, since I dumped him. We could have some one-last-time sex, and I could put something on him that would make him not want to marry Latrice and come running back to me. But then I wouldn't want him.

"Snap out of it, Candis. You sound like a fool," I said to my reflection in response to my thinking. "You know he doesn't want you. He never did. Remember?" Then I answered myself back. "Yeah, I do. I remember. You're right."

Turning the water on and pumping soap into my palms, I replaced Russell's scent with a cucumber-melon fragrance. I cupped my hands to my face again and sniffed, proud of myself, although the soap didn't smell nearly as good as he did.

"Did you see Russell?" Dina asked, practically attacking me once I came out of the bathroom.

"Russell who?" With my hand I dismissed the notion and walked off, but she stayed on my heels.

"Russell, your ex!" she exclaimed.

"So what? He's an ex, and he's engaged, or did you forget that?"

"Suppose they broke the engagement, though? I mean, he did show up here."

"Yeah, and I'm wondering how he knew to do that." I looked at her suspiciously while she picked up a piece of shrimp and stuffed it in her mouth. My hands flew to my waist, and I stared at her, demanding a response.

"It wasn't me." Dina shook her head quickly but still looked as guilty as sin. Adding a shrug, she said, "I don't know how he knew."

"Mmm-hmm," I murmured in disbelief. "You and Celeste are trying to be slick. Where is she?" I let my eyes dart around the room, looking for the other suspected accomplice in Russell's sudden and unexpected appearance. She was giggling and smiling all in the face of the guy she'd invited out on the dance floor as they did the cha-cha slide. I slid on out there right beside her, fell into step, and semi-yelled over the music, "I need to talk to you when this song is over."

"Okay." She grinned while she dipped and turned. Before I could ease my way off the floor, the DJ started playing 50 Cent's "In Da Club."

Everybody started shouting, "Go! Go! Go, Candis. It's your birthday! Go, Candis. It's your birthday," prompting me to stay on the dance floor and shake my groove thang. We ended up forming a *Soul Train* dance line right after that, and I must have danced to about ten songs consecutively before I couldn't take any more. I didn't think about Russell again until the end of the party, when we were cleaning up and putting gifts in my car.

Most of the gifts I'd received, I'd opened as soon as they were handed to me, but I took a second look at everything, anyway. I was consolidating bags of shoes, purses, various gift cards, jewelry, envelopes stuffed with cash, and little knickknacks, when I saw a small glossy black bag that I didn't remember seeing before. There was a card in the bag and a small box wrapped with a silk white ribbon, which begged me to open it. When I did, I gasped like I was having an asthma attack.

"Look at these!" I called to Celeste and Dina, who were washing some dishes in the kitchen. I didn't give them a chance to come to where I was. I grabbed the box with the pair of one-carat diamond studs and rushed toward the kitchen. They both dried their hands long enough to peer over at the earrings like they were newborn twins.

"Where did they come from? Somebody had some money!" Celeste squealed.

I slid my finger through the glued seal of the card's envelope, pulled the card out, and skipped all the reading to look at who'd signed it.

You're a diamond. As brilliant as you are, I was just too blind to see it.
Hope this makes up for all the bad times,
Russell

Chapter 22

Candis

Texting was my first inclination to thank Russell for the earrings, but I didn't know if the future Mrs. Wayne checked his phone, or if it would trip him up any other kind of way, which was not my intention. With that in mind, I semi-reluctantly called his number, assuming that I'd find him at work since it was ten o'clock on a Monday morning. He answered after two rings.

"I called to thank you for the beautiful birthday gift."

"You're welcome. I hope you like them."

"I love them," I gushed, touching my earlobes to make sure the earrings were still there.

"You deserve them. I should have gotten them for you a long time ago."

"What made you get them for me now?"

"I don't know." He paused for a couple of seconds. "I knew your birthday was coming up, and I started thinking about how things ended between us, and I guess I just kinda wanted to make it up to you."

"Make what up to me?"

"Make up the fact that I was too selfish to give you what you wanted and what you deserved."

At a loss for words, I didn't respond, and silence fell between us for a few seconds.

"I messed up," he admitted.

"I hear you're engaged now."

"Yeah," Russell sighed. "I wish it were you, though."

That caught me off guard, but I quickly recovered. "You could have made it me, but that's not what you wanted."

"I should have made it you," he mumbled.

"But you didn't."

"I tried to call you so many times, Candis, and you refused to take my calls. I need to see you," he stated, and immediately I had mixed emotions.

"I don't think that would be a good idea, Russell."

"Just for closure," he threw in. "There're just a few things I want to tell you, and I'd rather it be face-to-face."

"And what about Latrice? She's going to be fine with that?"

"You don't have to be concerned about that."

It was against my better judgment, but I did have the man's earrings stuck in my ears. And it would be nice to see him again while I held the upper hand and wouldn't be on the begging end of the spectrum. Hell, maybe I would stand him up.

"I guess I could squeeze in about fifteen minutes or so tomorrow morning. My schedule is slammed," I said.

"Fifteen minutes? I'll have to rush, but if that's all you can spare, I guess I'll have to make do."

We solidified plans for him to drop by before work the next day and share whatever it was that was on his heart. My plan was to be grateful for the studs, but then to be cold and indifferent. I wanted to let him know that I was angry with him for rejecting me, then asking another woman to marry him. As much as I wanted to act like I didn't want to hear anything he had to say, I desperately wanted to know why I wasn't good enough for him. What made Latrice so much better than me.

He didn't deserve the effort, but I wanted to show him how good I looked and what he was missing out on. At the same time, I couldn't have him thinking I'd gotten dressed up for him, but I needed to look sexy, carefree, and in control. Which was why, after my shower, I decided against the dress and pulled on a pair of pink sweatshorts that barely covered my booty and a wife beater. My skin was slathered in cocoa butter, giving me a natural glistening glow, and my hair was pushed back from my forehead with a headband. A touch of mascara made my eyes pop but didn't make me look made up, and I smoothed cherry lip balm across my lips just in case our lips happened to meet.

I caught myself constantly peeking out the window in anticipation of his arrival. I hated that I did that, but I couldn't seem to stop myself. He pulled up right before seven, then called me from the parking lot.

"Hey, Candis. I'm outside."

"Oh. I forgot you were coming. You'll have to excuse the way I'm dressed," I lied.

"It's all good."

"Just let yourself in," I offered, taking a seat on the couch and pushing toe separators between my toes to make it look like I'd been busy pampering myself. A minute later, he twisted the knob and pushed the door open.

"Hey," he greeted. His cologne swept across my nostrils as he entered, dressed in pair of loose-fitting jeans and a black graphic tee designed with a series of eagles' wings. He looked like a tall, cold glass of chocolate milk just waiting to be gulped down. Lord, have mercy, Russell was fine! If I wasn't trying to be in control, I would have thrown my arms around his neck, jumped up and circled his waist with my legs, and let him slam me against the front door and take me right there. My, my, my!

"Hey. Have a seat." Russell hesitated until I pointed to the chair directly across from me.

"So how've you been?" he asked, leaning forward on his elbows and clasping his hands.

"Good." I didn't look up at him but acted as if my toes were the most amazing things I'd seen in a long time.

"You look good." I saw him nod in my peripheral.

"Thanks."

"Those earrings look nice on you."

"Yeah. I love them," I commented with a smile, this time letting my eyes meet his while I touched my right earlobe. "Thank you again."

"You're welcome."

"So what is your future wife going to say when she finds out that you purchased some diamonds and they weren't for her?"

"I bought those earrings for you a long time ago, Candis," he answered. "I just never had an opportunity to give them to you, because . . . well, I guess you'd made a decision that we were done or, I should say, you were done with me."

"I had to draw the line somewhere, Russell. I wasn't willing to live my life hoping that one day you were going to come around."

"I understand. I wasn't ready."

"But now suddenly you are, and you're ready with someone else." I smirked in sarcasm, shook my head, and added another coat of polish to my nails.

"Because you wouldn't have me. I know you don't believe this, but I've missed you, Candis. I've thought about you every single day."

"So how is it that you can be engaged to another woman if your mind is stuck on me?"

Russell shrugged. "You'd walked out of my life, and she walked in. We started hanging out, and the next thing I know, she was planning a wedding."

"And you just went along with it?"

"I guess you could say that."

"So you never proposed to her?"

"I mean, I did, but we were kinda playing around, and she took it seriously. I didn't even have a ring. Hell, she bought her own."

"She bought her own engagement ring?" I asked, gawking.

He nodded instead of verbally responding.

Sista girl was *that* desperate? "She didn't know you were playing?"

"I guess not, because she started telling her family and all that."

"So she is bullying you into marrying her," I said and laughed. "And you're letting her. That's definitely not the Russell I know." Seemed like I did everything I knew how to do to get Russell to commit to a relationship with me, with no results, and come to find out all I had to do was just start planning a wedding. "And you're going to go through with it?" I asked when he didn't comment.

"I guess. The woman I really love has given up on me."

"And what woman is that? You can't be talking about me, because you never loved me."

"I've always loved you, Candis."

"Yeah, right." I guffawed as I remembered I had on booty shorts, stood to my feet, and stomped to the kitchen, with my toes pointed to the ceiling in an effort to not mess them up. "You want something to drink?"

"What do you have?" Russell stood and followed me but kept a respectable distance.

"Water, orange juice, grapefruit juice, coffee . . ."

"A little orange juice would be nice."

I pulled two glasses from the cabinet, gave them a quick rinse, and filled them halfway with orange juice. Handing him a glass, I lifted mine slightly in a mock toast. "Here's to letting go of the past." I leaned back against the counter, not taking my eyes off of Russell, trying to read his face. I thought I saw disappointment and defeat, and I loved it. With a slightly raised brow, I sipped from my glass.

"So it's good-bye for us, huh?" he asked, not having swallowed any juice yet.

"It was good-bye for us when I last said good-bye, Russell."

"Don't make this the end for us, Candis. It doesn't have to be this way. I love you, and I know that you love me still."

I brought my glass back up to my face to give me some time to think of how I wanted to respond. I did love Russell, but I wasn't about to admit that. And just because he wasn't really into Latrice didn't mean that he'd suddenly be interested in me. At the same time, he did call and text me every day for two months straight after our trip to Jamaica, but I ignored every single one of his voice mails and text messages. I wanted to believe him, but I couldn't.

"I think it's time for you to go." I nodded.

Russell sighed. "Candis . . ."

"Russell, I'm done." We stared at each other in an unspoken contest of who would look away first. It lasted fifteen seconds or more before Russell dropped his head.

"Baby, don't do this to us," he whispered, sitting his glass down on the countertop and coming toward me.

Instead of backing up, I let him wrap his arms around my waist while he studied my eyes. A fire ignited on my flesh from the warmth of his hands and the gentleness of his touch. I shifted nervously in his arms, not trying to get away, but trying not to get any closer for fear that the spring on my goody box might suddenly give way and then it would be on! And since I hadn't quite forgotten about the ass whuppin' I took from Chad's wife a few years ago, I wasn't exactly trying to find out if Latrice would or would not fight over her man.

"There is no *us*, Russell. There never was." I pushed against his chest as I stepped backward. "I'm sure your fiancée is looking for you."

Without saying a word, Russell picked up his glass, gulped the liquid in its entirety, then turned on his heels and walked out the door, leaving me standing in the kitchen.

This time as I watched him walk to his car, I didn't feel less than. I felt empowered and strong. I felt in control and was proud of myself for not folding and not selling myself for the price of a pair of earrings.

"Expect a package tomorrow, baby." That was the last thing SeanMichael said to me before we ended our Skype call the night before. Just as he'd said, a box arrived via FedEx shortly after Russell left. I sat down at my dining room table, scissors in hand, and cut through the packaging tape.

The first thing I opened was an envelope that held a card with a bouquet of roses on the front.

Dear BabyThang,
Though we've never met in person, I feel as if I know you well. I knew from the start that there was something beautiful and wonderful about you; you gripped my heart and wouldn't let go. Our relationship, though at a distance, has given me a lot of

peace and comfort, and I have yet to see you. You make me feel almost complete, and I say "almost" only because the only thing missing is your presence. You magically entered my life and filled me with the love of a lifetime. Now, each day I look forward to seeing you–even if from afar–talking with you, and blowing you kisses. You are what I want. You are who I want. I feel so special knowing that you love me. I'm so elated that we're able to share our love with each other in such a pure way. It truly seems as if you're a part of me, as if our meeting was orchestrated by the heavens. The thought of you fills me with feelings I can't even describe.

Physically, we're miles apart, but you're not far away from me at all. You're in my heart every day, always on my mind. Even though we are separated by miles, we're not apart at all, because during the day, we see the same beautiful sunshine, and at night we gaze at the same stars. I don't care how long it takes me to get to you and what I have to do until I can be there, but until I do, I blow kisses to the wind and command them to travel the beautiful airways until they land gently on your face. Until I can kiss you in person, I will fix my eyes on your picture and pray for you every night, before I go to sleep. I can't wait for these lonely nights to be over, and for my arms to be filled with you.

I love you with my whole heart, and no one can ever make me feel the way that you do. I'll always put you first. I'll take care of you and treat you like the queen that you are. There is no one else for me. You are the woman of my dreams, the queen of my soul, and the love of my life. You're the one who's right for my life, and I want us to take this journey into the rest of our lives together. Nothing would make me happier than for you to allow me to take your hand in marriage, as your husband, and to love you for the rest of our lives.

Candis Lorraine Turner, my sweet BabyThang, will you marry me?

Anxiously awaiting your answer,
SeanMichael Monroe

Beneath the card was a large fluffy yellow robe with a wide black ribbon tied around it and a handwritten note that said "Untie this ribbon." With a smile of expectation, I carefully untied the ribbon and unrolled the robe on the table. In the center was a red velvet box, which made my stomach tumble with butterflies.

"Here we go," I said to myself. I held my breath as I lifted the lid to the hinged box to reveal my ring.

What had been a grin of high hopes quickly turned into a frown of disappointment. SeanMichael had told me that he couldn't afford to get me the ring I truly wanted, but I was expecting a little bit more than what sat in the crease of that box in front of me. To say I was disappointed was an understatement. The ring looked like it was made of Cracker Jack gold instead of white gold, and the stone was so small, it was comparable to a single stud from a baby's pair of earrings. *What the hell?*

I stared at the ring for ten minutes with tears streaming down my face, trying to talk myself into sliding it on my finger.

"What's important, Candis? The ring or the man?" I said out loud. "Stop being so materialistic." I inhaled deeply and pushed the ring past the knuckles of my third finger on my left hand. At least it was the right size. Still, I was embarrassed to show it to anybody. I already knew SeanMichael would be crushed if I expressed anything but complete elation. Knowing this, I practiced gushing in the mirror for twenty minutes before I called him.

"Did you get it?" he asked as soon as he answered.

"It's beautiful, baby. I love it." I lied, hoping it was convincing.

"I'm sorry it's not exactly what you wanted."

"SeanMichael, I want you, and as long as I have that, I have exactly what I want." I cooed, and I did mean it. A nicer ring would have been great too, though.

"I love you, girl," he said with a sigh of relief.

"I love you too, baby."

"I gotta go. I'm at work, and we're pretty busy."

"Okay. Call me later."

"Hey, post a picture of your hand to Facebook, so I can let the world know that you're mine!" he said before ending the call.

Oh God.

That evening, with my mini ring on my finger, I headed for Celeste's apartment, our meeting place for the night. Not only was I excited about my engagement news, but I also was determined to get to the bottom of their matchmaking shenanigans.

"So which one of you two wenches tried to reset me up with Russell?"

Celeste and Dina knew this was coming and had ample time to build up their defenses. Dina obviously had none.

"It was Celeste's idea," she blurted.

I eyed Celeste, waiting for an explanation.

"What?" She hunched her shoulders nonchalantly.

"Why did you do that? You know I ended things with Russell months ago, and even more so, you know I'm seeing SeanMichael."

"*Seeing?* Is that what it's now called when you can only in-box, text, Skype, and make phone calls? From what I thought, you ain't seen him yet," Celeste replied, poking a little fun.

"Don't try to be funny. You know what I mean."

"No, I don't, because every guy I ever called myself seeing, I've actually been able to put my hands on him. I don't know what this mess is you call yourself doing," Celeste said, fanning her hand at me and rolling her eyes.

"Well, I was going to wait to tell you this, but just so y'all won't waste your time scheming and carrying on, I might as well go ahead and tell you now. . . ."

Chapter 23

Celeste

"SeanMichael and I are getting married," Candis announced to Dina and me before taking a swig of wine.

"SeanMichael who?" I blurted out, dropping my head and raising my eyebrows at the same time. "Please tell me you met another man named SeanMichael and you're not talking about that dude you met on Facebook."

"Are you serious, Candis?" Dina added right after me.

Candis rolled her eyes at me and focused on Dina. "Yes, I'm serious. We're getting married."

"And you've never met him?" I said, more as a statement, maintaining my dropped-face look.

"Not in person. We just got finished saying that."

"And you're *still* going to marry him?" I shook my head. "That don't make no damn sense."

"And I guess it made sense for you to marry Equanto," she shot back.

"No, it didn't, but at the very least, I did meet him and date him first."

"And that should have been all the reason not to marry him, from what you've shared with me." Candis poked her lips out and rolled her eyes.

See? That was why I didn't like sharing stuff with Candis and Dina half the time. Eventually, it got thrown back in my face.

***

Call me the queen of desperate, bored, or lonely, but Equanto and I met on a phone chat line, of all places. It started off as something fun and simple: dial a number, talk to a guy to pass some time, or in my case, to feel like somebody was interested in me again after David knocked me up during a one-night stand and left me with a baby, an extra hundred pounds, a stomach that had so many stretch marks it looked like a map of Africa, and self-esteem that was in the toilet. I couldn't deny that my baby, Linwood, was the love of my life, but I didn't need just love. I needed lovin'.

Equanto and I started talking every night on the chat line's coded number. One of the first questions he asked was, "So what do you look like?" It reminded me of just how out of shape I was, and it was a question I would have much rather avoided.

"Like a woman," was my answer. That meant I had curves and bulges that only a real man would appreciate.

He chuckled first. "Well, I hope you don't look like a damn man, but tell me something more than that."

"So where do you work?" I threw in as a distraction.

"We can talk about all that later," he said. "I bet you sexy as hell, though."

I wanted to give him a description of a bombshell body: nice, round, perky tatas; a flat belly; a curvy, thick behind; a tiny waistline; and long, flowing hair, like the females the chat line used in their commercials. This description was something that I thought he would take interest in, but all I could honestly lay claim to was the long, flowing hair, complements of my daddy's genes.

"I don't like to be vain like that," I said, dodging. "Beauty is in the eye of the beholder."

"You ain't tryin'a answer, so you must be fat, then,"
he said and guffawed.

I should have hung up the phone right then, but
instead, the conversation continued and we not only
exchanged our personal numbers but also agreed to
meet at the end of the week, after texting each other
head shots. The one I sent had most of my face hid-
den by my hair and showcased sexy bedroom eyes.
The one he sent me was an average shot of him sitting
on a couch with a half grin, half snarl on his face. He
would do.

That Saturday night Dina agreed to keep my baby
while I went out on my first date in three years,
with high expectations of making a love connection.
I tugged on a pair of denim-looking leggings and
a stretchy green one-shouldered top that was long
enough to cover my behind and was adorned with
large yellow and turquoise butterflies on the front.
My eye shadow and lip gloss matched the hues in my
shirt, and I flatironed my hair so that it framed my
face. Posing in the mirror, I gave myself two thumbs-
up; I looked good and was ready.

We'd decided to meet at Myst, a nightclub out in
Scottsdale, since it would provide a mixed crowd,
drinks, and hopefully a good time even if he didn't
work out, since Candis was coming with me for safety
reasons. We'd been at the club for more than an hour,
with me scanning every dude in my line of vision,
wondering if he was Equanto. In the meantime, I
danced with a couple of guys, but I was distracted,
scared I was going to miss him. I couldn't dance like
I really wanted to, because I didn't want to be sweaty
and stank by the time Equanto got there. That is, if he
wasn't standing me up.

Candis looked like she was having the time of her life, accepting drinks from all kinds of dudes, hoochie dancing—bending over, rubbing her booty all in guys' crotches—then blowing them off like nothing had ever happened when the song changed. I envied her freedom of expression, her confidence, and how guys just flocked to her. She had on a super minidress that flared out at the waist but fell just an inch below her cheeks.

At one point, she started doing some fast-paced dance that looked like a mix between Chicago stepping and the Hustle, which called for a few quick spins. Every time Candis did a spin, her dress flew up to her waist and showed off her perfectly round, incredibly toned ass, complete with a strip of thong up the middle. She knew it and didn't care. That girl danced like she owned the place, while guys stood all around with a hand cupped over their mouth, muffling their "Gahdahm!" while their other hand molested their crotches.

"Whew!" she huffed with a smile when the song ended and the DJ played something much slower. She made her way back to where I sat, and dudes started coming out of the woodwork like roaches with more drinks, requests for dances, and slips of paper with phone numbers scribbled on them, which she discarded.

While she sat chatting with someone to whom she'd decided to give two minutes of her attention, Equanto called.

"Yo, where you at?" he said.

I told him where to find me and described my outfit, and a minute later I saw an acceptable-looking man come strolling to the table.

"W'sup?" he said with a head bob, rubbing his hand across his face, looking back and forth between me and Candis.

"Humph," Candis grunted, rolling her eyes away in instant disapproval. "I'll be back." At that she was back out on the dance floor.

"Hey," I greeted with a slight smile, taking note of his features, which reminded me of Usher's.

He pulled up a chair beside me, leaned back, and scanned the club. "So what's up?"

"Nothing much. Been getting my dance on while I was waiting for you to get here." I glanced at my watch to send the nonverbal message that I didn't appreciate him taking so long to show up.

"Yeah. Sorry 'bout that. I had got a li'l caught up with something," he answered while he thumbed a text message into his phone. Silence hovered between us for about two minutes, with me sipping my drink and him preoccupied with his phone. When he was done, he spoke again. "So stand up. Lemme see what you look like." He lustfully bit down on his bottom lip and glanced down at a huge chunk of my butt that spilled over the sides of my seat.

I pondered for a few seconds if I should attempt Candis's level of confidence by proudly strutting my stuff or if I should ask him if he was crazy for approaching me like that. I took an even lower road. "My feet hurt a little bit," I lied. "I don't feel like standing up."

"Oh, a'ight. Well, I'm 'bout to go dance, then."

"Wow. Not even gonna offer to buy me a drink first," I said to his back, loud enough for him to hear as he hadn't gotten too far away. He didn't even turn around. He headed to the bar first, leaned over to the bartender, and was served a bottle of beer. He took a swallow, then sat on the edge of a bar stool, bobbing his head, watching females, and licking his lips. Another minute passed before some big-booty chick *approached him and led him to the floor. While the girl shook and gyrated, Equanto did slow, fluid movements, keeping time with the rhythm but not putting forth much effort.*

"Where's your date?" Candis asked, plopping down beside me, out of breath.

"He's out there with some random chick. I'm ready to go. Come on."

"So it's not a love connection, huh?"

"Nope." Grabbing my keys and purse, I ducked out without letting him know I was leaving. He probably didn't give a damn, anyway.

Equanto didn't call me until three days later.

"What happened to you the other night?"

"You mean, you noticed that I'd left?"

"I came back to the table with a drink for you, and you were gone," he commented.

"Really?" I said sarcastically. "So what'd you do with it? Give it to the same chick you gave your attention to when you were supposed to be with me?"

"See, it won't even like that. You said your feet were hurting, and after paying twenty dollars to get in, I did wanna dance at least one time."

He had a good point; I did say that.

"Then I come back to talk to you, and you dipped on a brother. Didn't say you were leaving or nothing."

"Right."

"So maybe that wasn't a good place for us to meet, but look, I am tryin'a see you again."

After a little convincing, I agreed to dinner, even though I had to pick him up, since his car was allegedly in the shop. Then I ended up paying for our meals because he'd "accidentally" left his wallet at home. I was so desperate for male attention, and some was better than none—even if I had to pay almost every time we went out. It had been a mess of a relationship ever since but I had always tried to convince myself and others that it wasn't that bad.

It seemed like the whole world was against us from the start, primarily because Equanto couldn't seem to keep a job. It seemed like by the time he was on a job long enough to get a check with his name printed on it, he found something about the job that was so difficult to put up with that he just had to quit.

"It's too hot to be out there every day, cutting grass!"

"Ain't nobody gonna do all that for no minimum wage."

"They want to start too early in the morning, and I'm not a morning person."

"I'm tryin'a work in my destiny, and this ain't it."

"Last time I went to church, the preacher said he seen albums with my name on it."

"I'm wasting my life making another man rich."

"My boss be trippin', and he ain't gonna be talking to me like that." He tagged that on to every main reason as the secondary reason why he just couldn't work another day.

In the meantime, he had moved in with me, because his sister had put him out for no reason, or so he said. It was initially just supposed to be for a few nights— and on the couch—until he got himself together, but one night turned into the next, which turned into a week, then a month, and so on. During that time, he transitioned from the couch to my bedroom, and when I looked up, I had a live-in lover. It was shackin', as my momma called it, but I kept lying to myself, calling it "spending the night," but even my three-year-old knew better than that.

"Is Equanto coming home?" Linwood asked me one evening, when Equanto hadn't come in after work.

Linwood was used to playing video games with him every night after dinner, and it was now almost his bath and bedtime.

"This is not his home, baby," I answered. "He's just spending the night here for a little while."

"Oh. I thought he lived here with us."

Hell, who was I fooling? He did live there with us, and I was pissed off that I hadn't heard from him all evening and had no idea where he was. I felt like he owed me an explanation out of respect.

It was after eleven when he stuck his key in the lock and twisted the knob. The first thing I saw was a bouquet of mixed flowers, which immediately broke my angry spell. Equanto had never brought me flowers before.

"I'm sorry I'm late. They was offering extra hours, and I had to get that overtime."

"You couldn't call me?"

"My phone was dead, babe," he said, offering the blacked-out, nonresponsive device as proof. The job he was currently working, a car detailing gig, paid him under the table, so he dug into his pocket and pulled out a small wad of folded bills and handed them to me. "Here's some money for letting me stay with you."

That completely caught me by surprise. Equanto would pick up a few groceries here and there or pay for dinner if we went out, but he'd never put money in my hand before. That kinda made him an official tenant, except he wasn't on my lease. And I couldn't even front. When he wasn't working, he saved me a few dollars by keeping Linwood while I worked, instead of me having to take him to day care.

"Don't worry about li'l man. He can stay here with me," he'd said. Anybody with a kid knew that someone who was willing to keep your kid for free was a plus.

Then he didn't mind cooking on top of that, although the meals were fairly simple: spaghetti, hot dogs and fries, fried chicken with boxed mashed potatoes and canned green beans. He got no complaints from me, and I found myself making excuses for his lack of employment to Candis and Dina.

"It works better for us this way, 'cause I don't have to pay child care. And he does the laundry and stuff."

"So he's the damn woman in the relationship," Candis observed.

"Only if you think about it in terms of traditional gender roles, but this is not the nineteen fifties anymore," I argued, defending myself.

"Well, get his ass an apron, then," Candis replied.

"It's just what works for us."

"But the Bible says a man who doesn't work doesn't eat." Dina was always trying to put a church spin on stuff, but I had an answer.

"It also says in Proverbs thirty-one, which is supposed to be about the perfect woman or something like that, that she goes to work and makes her man proud of her."

"When have you ever read that!" Dina exclaimed. "I gotta Bible right here in my purse."

"Turn to it." I challenged. She did, and after reading all that stuff that the woman did, spinning wool and planting vineyards and selling linen and whatnot, there wasn't a whole lot she could say about me working.

"But you ain't married to him," Candis shot back. She always had something negative to say. "It would be one thing if he was your husband, but ain't no way in the world I would carry a grown-ass man on my back."

Now, there wasn't a whole lot I could say about that. Regardless, what did my stupid ass do? Shortly after that conversation with the girls, I proposed to him after we'd finished making love.

"E, I'm not comfortable living like this," I said.

"Like what, baby?" He was still lying on me, breathing softly in my ear.

"You living here, lying up in my bed every night, and we're not married. Especially in front of my son."

"So what're you saying? You want me to get out your house?"

"No. I want to get married."

Equanto grunted, "I don't know about all that." He lifted his weight and slid to his side of the bed.

"Why not?"

"'Cause."

I waited for him to say more, but nothing else followed.

"Because what? We're already living like we're married. I need to put the right kind of relationship example in front of my son . . . and I love you."

Even if he was still going to say no to marriage right now, I did expect him to say that he loved me too. He didn't say it.

"I don't know about all that, Celeste." He turned his back to me and dozed off, while I lay there disappointed, hurt, and spilling tears on my pillow.

It seemed like things just really went downhill from there. I was used to him not keeping a job and being home most of the time, but it started to turn into extreme laziness, and I got impatient and angry. I'd come home from work, and he'd be sitting on my couch with the damn Wii remote in his hand, playing some stupid game, telling me what level he'd made it to and some new cheat code he'd discovered. On top of that, the house looked like a hurricane had come through, even though I'd straighten up every night, before I went to bed. Our bed wouldn't be made, and no kind of meal had been cooked. My baby was surviving off what I called the C food group—cereal, crackers, cheese puffs, chips, cookies, and Coolie drinks, all of which he could get for himself. Coming home to a lazy unemployed man was like getting off of one job and going straight to another. Except the one at home was twice as hard.

"You gonna have to go, Equanto," *I asserted one day, when I'd just reached my limit, coming home to find three other men in my house, around my baby, drinking beer and playing dominoes.*

"Why? Go where?"

"I don't care where you go, but you gonna have to get outta my house."

"Oh, so now it's your house by yourself?"

"Hell, yeah! You don't pay rent or nothing else around here!"

"Yeah, but I do other stuff," *he argued.*

"Like what?" *With my hands planted on my hips, I looked around the room. The trash hadn't been taken out, dishes were in the sink, which was a mystery, because nothing had been cooked. And beer cans were strewn on the floor, and the house smelled like stank feet, sweaty underarms, and musty balls.*

"I keep Linwood for you, and I cook and stuff sometimes."

"That ain't cutting it no more, E. You gonna have to get a job or get out my house."

"Well, you gonna have to take Linwood to day care so I can go fill out some applications."

"That ain't no problem!" *I snapped, but actually it was. I had long withdrawn him from the center he'd* been enrolled in, comfortable to some degree with him staying home with Equanto. I'd have to call them to see if they had room and then reregister him if they did. If not, I'd have to go day-care shopping, which was time consuming. Not to mention, the expense that I'd gotten used to not having to pay. Oh well. I was doing things on my own before I met Equanto, and I could sure as hell carry on without him now.

By the time we went to bed that night, he had calmed down and wanted to talk.

"Baby, I am gonna look for a job tomorrow, but don't put me out of your and li'l man's lives. I know I can do better, but y'all like my family now. He's like my son."

"And what am I like, since you don't want to get married? Am I like your wife, or am I like your 'something to do till something better comes along?'"

"You know it ain't even like that."

"What I do know is, you don't love me, you don't want to marry me, you can't keep a job, you're not contributing anything to this household, and now you're letting your friends come up in here and sit on my furniture, watch my TV, eat up my food, inhale my air-conditioning, and run up my electric bill. And I'm supposed to be okay with that? You must be out of your mind!"

"I didn't think it was gonna bother you like that, babe."

"Whatever, E."

"And I been thinking about what you said about us living like we married and stuff, but I was raised in church and I know it ain't right. I was gonna ask you to marry me, but I was too ashamed, because I didn't have a ring to give you."

What? I was at a loss for words.

"I do love you, babe. I'm just trying to get myself together so I can be the man I need to be for you."

He said some more stuff that was pleasing to my ears, and in no time the panties were off and the legs were spread. Before the month was out, we went down to the justice of the peace and tied the knot, even though he was still unemployed, unmotivated, and un *everything else that I wanted my husband to be. Including unloving.*

My life had been hell on earth ever since, and Candis knew it. So why in the world would she want to jump up and marry a dude she met on freaking Facebook?

Chapter 24

Dina

As soon as Celeste closed the door behind Candis, we started up. "Do you think she's serious?" I asked with my brows lifted so high, it made my head hurt.

Celeste just stood at the door, one hand still on the doorknob and the other on her hip. "I sure hope not."

"I don't know, Celeste." I forked more lasagna in my mouth. "If she is, what are we going to do?"

"What can we do? Hopefully, that man will show his ass before this gets out of hand. Candis is too old to be acting this stupid."

"It's already out of hand if she is talking about marrying him," I replied, throwing up a hand and letting it come down on the table. "Don't you think so?"

"Kind of, but not really. With that bubble gum ring she got, maybe it's just a pretend engagement. You know, wishful thinking, a promise ring." Celeste meandered back to the living room, grabbed the remote from her coffee table, and took a seat. "He hasn't put a real ring on it."

"Did you hear her say he mailed her the ring?"

"Mailed it?" Celeste jerked her head toward me so fast, it was a miracle her neck didn't snap.

"She said he didn't have the money to come out here, but he didn't want her walking around with nothing on her hand, so he mailed it."

Celeste shook her head. "That doesn't even make good sense."

"Nothing about this whole thing makes any sense at all. I can't believe she is being so desperate. She needs to take her time and spend some time with him in person, not online."

"I know, right?"

"But, look, what are you going to say when she asks you to be in the wedding? Because you know she's going to ask," I said. We were Candis's best friends, so I was sure she'd be asking us to be bridesmaids.

"They probably won't have a wedding. I can't see them having one. It will probably be a justice of the peace thing like E and I did, if that."

"Are they planning on living here, or is she going to go out there?"

"She said she's moving to Baltimore," Celeste replied. "If she knows like I know, she better stay here, where she can get to some help if she needs it."

"I know that's right. You know how abusers do. They isolate you first, then go to whippin' your ass!" We both paused, pensive.

"She's going to snap to her senses," Celeste finally said, but she didn't really look like she believed what she'd said.

"Marriage is hard enough all by itself without adding all this extra drama to it. Trust me—"

"Wait a minute," Celeste interrupted. "He didn't have the money to fly out here and propose like a real man?"

"Nope."

"So if he ain't got the money for a plane ticket, how in the world he got the money to take care of a wife?"

"Exactly. That's what I was thinking. She'd be a fool to marry a broke-ass man, then move all the way across the country to live with him," I shot.

"Well, you can't live anyone's life but your own. I just hope he don't kill her," Celeste observed.

"We need to do something to talk her out of this mess."

"Something like what?"

"What happened with her and Hamilton? Maybe we need to try to hook them up again," I suggested.

"I don't think they ever kicked things off. The chemistry wasn't there." Celeste twisted a finger into her hair, pulled on the coil and let it spring back toward her head. "Well, I take that back. She gave him some of her hot chocolate, and he went on about his business."

"What about Russell?"

"Engaged Russell?" Celeste asked. "She just told us she dissed him."

"That's just for now. You know she loves him. We're gonna have to try to hook them up again."

"Yeah, right. And Candis would be mad at us for the rest of our lives," she said, pulling on more strands of hair.

"So? At least she'd still have a life to be mad about. It's worth a try. You know how sex with the ex can be. It might be just the thing she needs to come to her senses."

"Sex? See, you're going too far. Do you think his fiancée is going to agree to all that, just to keep Candis from marrying some pervert? She better be glad she doesn't have any kids, because he's probably a pedophile." Celeste stretched her eyes to emphasize her point. "But still it's not our place to try to control her relationship or mess up Russell's engagement. I'm still trippin' off the part that he mailed her the ring instead of coming to meet her. What kind of mess is that? Who ever heard of mailing somebody an engagement ring?"

Really Celeste couldn't talk, because Equanto hadn't put so much as a rubber band around her finger.

"Where did she say he worked at again?" I twisted my own engagement ring around my finger. "At a gas station, right?"

"Yeah, pumping gas and washing windows. He doesn't even have a good job. I don't mean no harm, but Candis needs some help."

"She need something!" I agreed with her.

"She needs to take it from me. Starting off on the wrong foot is not fun. She better learn how to appreciate her singleness and stay single," Celeste threw in, thinking about her own godforsaken marriage.

"We're never satisfied with where we are, because the grass always looks greener on the other side." I shook my head. "You know every single person wants someone to cuddle up with at night."

"Yeah and every married person is wondering what the hell were they thinking when they got married in the first place."

"Can't live with 'em, can't live without 'em."

"You got that right. I'd trade places with Candis in a minute to be single again." Celeste paused for a few seconds but decided to switch the subject before she fell into a depression behind Equanto and his drama. "So what's going on with you and Bertrand?"

"Please don't even get me started, Celeste. I'm trying to enjoy my evening."

Celeste was shocked to hear me respond that way. To her, Bertrand and I made the perfect couple, despite typical ups and downs.

"I'm just asking. I know you said y'all were going through a little something, but I didn't know it was like that."

"It's not just a little something." I shook my head and looked away. "I'm just about ready to break our engagement," I added, looking like I had a hard time forming the words and letting them leave my mouth.

"Girl, stop lying."

"I'm serious. I can't keep living my life being miserable, and I don't see how it's going to work out between us. I tried to get him to go to premarital counseling, and we went to one session and he quit. Didn't want to go anymore. I try talking to him, but he doesn't want to talk, so what am I supposed to do?"

"You're supposed to try to work it out."

"I've tried to work it out. I don't know what else I can do, and I'm tired of letting him ride my body but not work on our relationship, while I wash his nasty drawers, cook dinner, and keep the house clean. That's why he ain't got no coochie in almost two months now."

"Two months!" Celeste gasped.

"Yep. Two months."

"Dina, you know you can't put that man on sex restriction like that and think things are going to get better."

"Why can't I? Explain to me how it's right for him to get what he wants, pussy on demand, and I get nothing but hurt feelings. How exactly does that work?" My voice escalated, as my anger grew.

"Oh snap! You're mad for real huh?" Celeste paused and grinned while I silently scowled. "You didn't say kitty kat, Tootsie Pop or goody box like you normally say; you said pussy! You shonuff mad!" she chortled.

She was right, I was completely fed up. "But you have to know you're playing a dangerous game by not fulfilling that very important part of your duties."

"We aren't married, so I don't have any duties," I argued. "And even when I was fulfilling them, he snuck out here and decided to screw around."

"Did anything come out of the counseling?"

"I just told you, we only went to one session. Nothing came out of that except how much of a liar he is, sitting in there, acting like he was clueless as to why we were there, wouldn't admit any fault, just sitting there, looking dumb in the face. That's such an insult."

"So what did the counselor say?"

"What could he say when nothing of substance was being said? I expressed what my issues were—that I thought he was a controlling cheater—and Bertrand didn't say much of anything, even when the counselor posed questions."

"I know he just didn't sit in there and just stare at the man," Celeste replied.

"He might as well have, for all he said. 'I've not done anything wrong. Dina believes what she wants to believe,'" I said, trying to mock Bertrand's voice. "I just can't do it, girl. The towel is in my hand and ready to be thrown in. I mean, we're not married, so why struggle with something I don't have to deal with at all? We've not made any solid commitments or taken any vows. As a matter of fact, all I'm doing is living in sin. Why should I sit up here and risk going to hell for a shabby, ragtag relationship?"

Celeste sighed. "Just make sure that you think things through before you make any decisions."

"I have thought things through."

"Have you told Bertrand that you want to end things?"

"Yeah I have." I dropped my head like I was scared or ashamed.

"So why haven't you moved on if that's what you want to do?" Celeste challenged.

"I don't know, and there are some parts of me that are uncomfortable with that. I think some of it is fear."

"So in other words, you haven't made up your mind about what you want."

"I guess not," I said, sulking.

"You know that's not fair to Bertrand."

"I'm not concerned about what's fair to him right now. What he did wasn't fair to me. What he did didn't consider me, regard me, honor me, or respect me," I said almost growling.

"So is it your plan to just try to make him miserable?"

"Am I supposed to be miserable just so he can be happy? Is that what you're suggesting, Celeste?" I questioned with an attitude.

"No, I'm not saying that. I'm just saying, nobody is perfect. You are going to have to deal with something no matter who you choose to be involved with, and I really don't think Bertrand is all that bad. He's a good man."

"Good in what way?" I rolled my eyes.

"Hell! In what way is he *not* good? So what if he wants to hear from you all day and all that jazz? That mess is petty. He keeps a job and pays the bills. And all you gotta do is give him some extra attention. I'd trade Equanto for Bertand any day and do whatever he asked me to do. Cook, clean, drop it like it's hot, let him know where I'm at twenty-four hours a day. Girl, you are seriously trippin'."

"You're forgetting about how he cheated on me."

"So he made a mistake." Celeste shrugged. "It was one time. We all make mistakes. Forgive him, let it go, and move on."

"It's not that easy, Celeste. I don't know that it was one time. As far as I know, it could still be going on."

"Girl, please. I'd marry that man so quick, and if I found out he was cheating on me, he'd *really* be taking care of me, 'cause I'd divorce his ass, take half his stuff, and collect alimony."

"Not everybody wants to willingly put themselves through potential heartbreak," I noted.

"And obviously, not everybody recognizes a good man when he's right in the palm of her hand."

Chapter 25

Dina

When I got back from Celeste's house, after being hit with the shocking news that Candis was planning on marrying SeanMichael, and feeling confused about how to move forward-or not-with Bertrand, it was after ten, so to see Bertrand sitting on the front porch was unusual. His presence startled me initially, as I didn't expect his silhouette to appear in the dark. The porch light was off, and he just sat in silence, looking crazy in the face.

"Hey, babe," I said, walking up onto the porch.

"Hey," he said flatly.

"What are you doing out here? You scared me."

"Just thinking."

"Thinking about what? And why are you thinking out here in the dark?"

"Just needed some fresh air."

"Oh, okay. So what are you thinking about?"

"A little bit of everything." He kept his eyes focused forward, and his arms were folded across his chest.

"Like what?"

"Like why didn't you answer your phone when I called you?" His voice was low and even.

"Because I'd left it in the car to charge." That wasn't wholly true. I had left it in the car to charge, but after thirty minutes, I'd retrieved it. When I saw I'd missed Bertrand's call three times, I didn't bother to return it, knowing that he was going to act like he was acting at the moment . . . nasty. I figured I'd rather deal with it once I got home than have it ruin the evening with my girls, but I did call him once I'd gotten in the car and started for home. It did no good because he hadn't answered.

"You left it in there the whole time?"

"Yes," I lied. "I didn't need it while I was sitting in the house."

"So what was I supposed to think?"

"What were you supposed to think about what?"

"About my wife being out late and not answering her phone," he said, cutting his eyes at me.

I use to love it when he called me his wife but now I didn't want to hear it. It made me cringe inside. "You were supposed to think that I was at Celeste's house, like I told you. Why were you calling me, anyway? What was wrong?"

"I wanted to make sure nothing had happened to you, since you didn't call me and let me know you made it over there safely," he snapped.

"Bertrand, if something had happened to me, someone would have called you. Me, the police, the paramedics, the hospital, my momma, Candis, Celeste, somebody!" I said, throwing my hands in the air.

"So you couldn't be considerate enough to call me and let me know everything was all right?"

"I didn't realize there were required checkpoints set up for me, like I'm some kind of teenager. I thought I was grown." My tone was still calm, although I was becoming irritated.

"And you being grown does not negate the fact that you should be accountable to me. What are you going to do once we are married? As a married woman, why do you have a problem with letting your husband know where you are?"

"I told you where I was going two hours ago, when I left, Bertrand."

"Yeah. That was two hours ago. Then you don't answer your phone, and that's supposed to be okay," he said with sarcastic scorn.

"When I called you back, you didn't answer your phone, either, so it sounds like to me, the pot is calling the kettle black."

"But I'm sitting at home. You were out in the streets."

"So the rule is, if you are sitting at home, you don't have to answer your phone? Is that what you're saying?" He didn't answer, probably realizing how stupid that sounded. "This is crazy. I'm going in the house." I pushed the front door open, leaving Bertrand sitting on the porch by himself, and headed to bed.

A full hour passed before he came back inside, fumbled around in the kitchen, from what I could hear, then came to the bedroom. My back was turned to him as I pretended to be asleep, but I listened as he showered, then got in bed beside me but made sure that our bodies didn't touch.

All this over a missed phone call? *Whatever,* I thought to myself and drifted off to sleep.

The next morning Bertrand woke me up by pressing his manhood into my backside and kissing my left shoulder.

"Babe, you up?" he whispered. When I didn't answer, although I'd heard and felt him, he pressed his hips forward and wrapped his arm around my waist. "Dina," he called.

"I'm up," I mumbled.

Bertrand knew that I hated to be awakened from my sleep for sex, and most of the time he respected my request that he not do that. The fact that he woke me up regardless of that meant he was really horny and would bug me until I gave in. I sighed because I just couldn't help it, then rolled over on my back to let him in. Bertrand wasted no time shifting his weight atop my frame and burying his face into my neck. After a few seconds of fumbling around, trying to get himself correctly positioned, he held his breath as he eased into my body, then exhaled a moan. Slowly, he rocked his hips, then settled into a smooth cadence that woke up my insides. Wrapping my legs around his waist, I pulled him closer to me and worked my hips upward to meet his stroke.

"Oh, baby," he panted, speeding up his movements. "Girl, you feel amazing!" he gasped, tucking his head down to lap at my nipples, causing me to arch my back and caress his head, encouraging him to continue.

"Mmm," I moaned into his ear as I stroked his back with my other hand. Even when I didn't feel like engaging, Bertrand always brought me to the point where I enjoyed it immensely, sleepy or not. On his way to the finish line, he bore into me with more aggression, gripping my shoulders and breathing heavily into my ear. "Yeah . . . that's it, baby," I whispered. "That's it."

Unable to hold back, Bertrand's body contracted as he released and exhaled several times in satisfaction. "I love you, baby," he murmured, rising and falling against my chest and planting kisses on my right shoulder. "I love you, Dina."

Hearing him whisper those words with such sincerity after we made love always brought tears to my eyes. Those words would remind me of all that was missing in my prior relationships, then erase the pain of those memories of not feeling loved or wanted. They always brought healing to some inner part of me that still remembered what it felt like to be rejected, stepped on, and played for a fool. His words humbled me, because I thought Bertrand meant every word, and my heart was overwhelmed by his love, and by the fact that he found me worthy to share his love with. It was during one of those whispered moments that I fell in love with Bertrand.

Now I lay there crying, because I couldn't believe that he'd betrayed me by sharing himself with someone else. While Bertrand felt amazing physically, emotionally I was in turmoil. I didn't know what to do. Forge ahead in forgiveness and believe that he honestly and truly loved me, or shut the door on this whole thing.

With Bertrand's weight still keeping me pinned to the mattress, I thought about what Celeste had said, and tried to weigh the pros and cons of staying with Bertrand and going through with our wedding plans. Maybe I was making too much of whatever had happened, and honestly, I couldn't prove anything. The panties could have been old. The texts could have meant nothing. And Bertrand did apologize for how he'd made me feel. I guess that had to count for something.

Then I thought about his controlling behaviors. They were irritating, but were they completely intolerable? He could definitely teach me a few things about managing my finances if I just humbled myself a little bit and followed his lead. We got along for the most part . . . well, as long as I played by his rules. They weren't really that bad, were they? Call to let him know I was okay, check with him before spending cash, try a little harder to meet his expectations. I mean, they weren't completely unreasonable. We could make this work. Celeste was right. No one was perfect, and I needed to recognize that I had a good man and embrace him, flaws and all.

"You're gonna mess around and make me marry you," I whispered.

"I should hope so. You're wearing my ring."

"Yeah, I am, aren't I?" I giggled. "So how about next month?" The time frame was random and off the top of my head, but I was ready to move forward before I changed my mind. After all, I was sleeping with the man, and had been living with him way longer than I'd expected to.

"Next month? What kind of wedding are you planning that can be put together that quickly?"

"I was thinking a destination wedding. Maybe Cancún or Hawaii . . . or Paris!" I grinned.

"Paris would be nice. I've never been." Braced on his elbows, he hovered over me, dropping down for a kiss after a few seconds. "We'll have to look at how much it would cost. If we can do it for less than ten grand, and if that's what you want, that's fine with me." He kissed me once more, then lifted himself from my body, rolled to his side of the bed, and stood in a stretch. "We'll just have to do a reception for our friends and family when we get back to the States."

His manhood was now deflated and hung limply in front of him, but he was still sexy, with all kinds of cuts and muscle definition in his chest, abs, and thighs.

"You might want to put that away," I said, grinning, "before I jump out this bed and attack you."

"After what you just did to me, I don't think you're going to get anything else out of this for at least an hour or two, but you're welcome to jump in the shower with me and try it out."

He didn't have to invite me twice.

Thirty minutes later, we both were smiling from ear to ear, rushing around and bumping into each other in the bathroom, trying to get ready and be on time for work.

"You're amazing," he complimented, licking, then biting down on his bottom lip and swatting my butt. "That's you, babe." Bertrand had me just about turned upside down in the shower and had me gasping for breath and reaching for the walls, as if they would offer something for me to hold on to. There was no doubt about it; I was going to have to marry this man.

Bertrand walked me out to my car, holding my coffee cup, like he did every morning. He opened my car door, let me get settled inside, then handed me my coffee. "All right, baby, have a great day," he said, leaning in for a kiss.

"Ooh, I forgot my phone. Can you go get it for me real quick? I left it in the kitchen, right beside the coffeepot."

"Sure." While I waited for Bertrand to return, I pulled the car out of the driveway and shifted it into gear, ready to take off.

"I don't see it," he yelled from the door to the curb.

"Did you look on the table?"

"It's not there, babe." With his lips turned down, he shook his head.

"All right, I'll get it when I get home. I don't have time to look for it. Love you!"

"Love you too." He waved as I pulled off.

At least I didn't have to worry about him blowing my phone up all day while I worked.

Chapter 26

Candis

With a few camera tricks, special lighting and photo editing, I was able to make my ring look amazingly huge and brilliant, as if a hundred-watt light bulb was sitting on my finger. It took less than an hour to have a ton of Facebook 'likes' and comments for the photo of my hand now dressed with an engagement ring.

Dina Winston, Celeste Parker and 57 other people like your photo.
Congratulations!
I didn't know you were getting married!
What! I'm so happy for you!
It's beautiful! Congratulations!
May God bless your union.
You two make a beautiful couple. Happy for you.
I'll be looking for my invite!
In-box! Now!

The comments went on for the rest of the day, with me having to explain to several people that, yes, I'd been seeing someone, and, yes, he was from Baltimore. I avoided saying that he lived there and just stuck to the fact that he was from there. More and more, I was getting the question of why there was no picture of the two of us together.

"Because I've not posted any yet," I answered. It wasn't a lie.

Dina and Celeste were taking me out that coming weekend to celebrate my engagement, although I knew they weren't completely comfortable with my decision. They were just going to have to learn to shut up, because I wasn't going for anyone down talking my man. He was my man, my sweetheart, my honey, whether they liked it or not. I could tell by the look on their faces and their patronizing congratulations that they were covering their true thoughts.

"Your ring is nice," Dina had commented unconvincingly, while Celeste had kept her comments to herself. It was better that way.

"Thanks. It's not the one I wanted," I'd felt obligated to explain, "but the ring doesn't make the marriage." Dina had the Rock of Gibraltar on her finger, while Equanto had never presented Celeste with a ring, and both of them were unhappy in their relationships. Really, I thought Celeste was jealous, but just because her husband wouldn't do right by her wasn't motivation for me to let her rain on my parade.

I'd been in the studio, editing shots of photos, for the past two hours and was ready to go grab something for lunch when the front door chime alerted me that someone had walked in. My heart just about stopped beating when I saw it was Latrice Chambers with a crazy-looking, cheap front lace wig on and a not-so-pleasant look on her face. *Oh, snap!* She was dressed in a too-small pink T-shirt that barely stretched over her belly, a white broomstick skirt, and pink heels that were too high for her to walk in comfortably, judging from the way she wobbled toward me. Her pinkie toes hung over the sides and touched the floor, and had I not been terrified, I would have bust out laughing.

"My name is Latrice Chambers, and your ex-boyfriend Russell is my fiancé, and I want to know what the hell is going on between you and him," she demanded, holding a Coach look-alike bag on her arm.

"Excuse me?" I answered.

"I want to know what is going on between you and Russell." She hadn't raised her voice, but she stretched her eyes and twisted her neck so much, she looked like Woodsy Owl.

"There's been nothing between myself and Russell in a very long time," I responded, easing behind my reception counter and inconspicuously pushing a panic button. Latrice wasn't dressed for a fight, but that didn't mean she didn't have intentions to kick her shoes off and throw blows, a weapon in her bag, or a posse of girls waiting just outside the door, ready to rush in at her command. I couldn't take any chances.

"That is not what he's telling me."

Oh, God. What had Russell said, and why hadn't he given me some kind of heads-up? Maybe he didn't know she was even here.

"Miss, I don't know you, but I assure you that there was never much of anything between myself and Russell, and I have no connections with him right now."

"When is the last time you seen him?"

I couldn't stand in front of this woman and admit to her that Russell had been at my house only a couple of weeks ago, after coming to my birthday party. Had he told her about the earrings too? Thank goodness I didn't have them on today, although I'd worn them consistently since he'd given them to me. It just so happened that I'd taken them off to clean them and mistakenly left them on my dresser.

"I've not seen him in a long while," I answered, which wasn't a lie. How long was a while? That could be thirty minutes if you were outside waiting for the city bus or fifty years ago.

"Hold up, 'cause I'm fin-na get to the bottom of this," she said, digging through her purse and pulling out her cell phone. "I'm 'bout to call his lying ass right now." She pushed a few buttons, then perched a hand on her hip.

Come on, Russell. Have my back. If he ever felt an ounce of love for me, now was the time he could prove it. *Deny everything. Where are the damn cops!*

"Hello," I heard him say, even though she held the phone up to the side of her face.

"Russell!" she barked.

"What, Latrice?" I overheard.

"I'm standing right here in front of your ex-girlfriend, and I need for you to tell me what you said earlier." She focused her eyes on me, letting them travel down my body, as if she were sizing me up.

"You where?" his muffled voice buzzed from her phone.

"Down here at this photography studio where she work at."

"What the hell are you doing there, Latrice? You're always trying to start some drama!"

"I told you I was coming down here, 'cause I know your ass is lying," she said into the phone.

"Latrice, get out that girl's shop."

"Nope, not till I find out what's going on."

"I already told you ain't nothing between me and her," I heard him say, and for the first time I released a breath, although my fear was still very present. I was just glad to have not heard him say he was at my house the other week and that he'd given me a birthday gift.

"So why I done heard three times that you were all up in her house and whatnot?"

I couldn't imagine Dina sharing with Latrice that Russell had given me diamonds, and I hadn't told either one of them that he'd come over, so how did Latrice know all this? I let out a huge sigh when finally two police cruisers drove into the lot and slowed to a stop. They weren't moving fast enough for my taste, looking at the front of the building, all confused. Finally, they opened the door to the studio and glanced around, looking for danger, I was sure.

"Everything okay in here, ma'am?" the first officer asked, bouncing his eyes between me and Latrice.

"Hold on, Russell. Hold on. I know she didn't call the damn cops on me," I heard her mumble under her breath as a look of panic crossed her face. "It ain't nothing going on, Officers," she said to the policemen before I could say anything, but they looked at me to confirm her statement before they took her word.

I didn't just want to break crazy on the girl and have her carted off downtown, just in case she knew where I lived, since she seemed to know so much. I had to think quickly on my feet.

"There was a bit of commotion outside," I began, "and I saw a bunch of guys running through here real wild and noisy. It was just myself and my client here in the store." I glanced over at Latrice. "And since it was just us two females, I figured I'd rather us be safe than sorry," I added.

Latrice looked down in her purse for a few seconds, which gave me a few seconds to signal one of the officers with my eyes that I was lying and was scared as hell of my so-called client. He acknowledged my response with a quick nod, cutting his eyes over to Latrice.

"I was hoping that you could see us both to our vehicles," I said.

"Yes, ma'am. Are there any other entrances to your studio?"

"There's a back door, but it is securely locked," I answered.

"Let me just take a look at it, if you don't mind."

"Not at all." While he traveled to the back and the other officer used his radio to communicate some codes to the dispatcher, I looked over at Latrice. "If you come in here again, I'm sending your ass to jail," I snarled, barely moving my lips.

Latrice was escorted to her car first, while one of the officers got a clear story from me of what really happened.

"Ma'am, I would recommend that you keep your door locked and install a bell for your clients."

"Yes, sir," I answered.

As soon as I was safely in my car, I called SeanMichael.

"Babe, I need you to come on out here quick!" I rushed. Although I was no longer in danger, I was still nervous and a bit shaky.

"What's wrong?" he asked.

Right before I started, I contemplated if I should tell him about Russell giving me diamonds. That might not go over well; I didn't want to be accused of sneaking around with my ex. It was definitely as risky as Truth or Dare? I decide to go with the truth, starting with, "My ex-boyfriend's fiancée came to the studio today, asking me what was going on between him and me, and I had to call the cops."

"Are you all right?" he asked.

I heard the tension in his voice. "Yeah, I am now. I'm going to be keeping that front door locked all the time now and just keeping a sign on the door telling people to knock."

SeanMichael fell silent for a few seconds before speaking again.

"Why did she come up there?"

"I don't know, babe. I have no idea. I've only seen her a few times in the shop where Dina works. I've never even really spoken to her."

"She had to have a reason to come up there. I mean, evidently you did something."

"What do you mean, evidently I did something? How do you figure it was me? Why couldn't it be that Russell did something to provoke her coming up here?" I asked, offended at what felt like an accusation.

"Okay, then, what did Russell do?" he asked, his tone becoming more aggressive.

"I really don't know," I answered, and really I didn't. I had no idea what Russell had said to Latrice to prompt her visit.

"I'm not calling you a liar, Candis, but I don't believe you."

"What reason do I have to lie to you, SeanMichael?"

"I don't know. You tell me," he ordered. "You're saying your ex's fiancée showed up at your place of business out of the clear blue sky, and you have no idea what made her do that. That just doesn't sound like the truth to me."

"So you're calling me a liar," I stated, but I meant it as a question.

"I am asking you to tell me the whole truth."

"I told you I don't know what Russell did or said to his fiancée. I mean, Russell showed up to my birthday party, but I asked him to leave."

SeanMichael didn't speak a word.

"Hello?"

"I'm here," he answered in a growl. Then there was silence for another thirty seconds. "So your ex-boyfriend showed up at your birthday party, and you didn't even tell me."

"It really wasn't a big deal." I shrugged, although he couldn't see me.

"Who invited him, Candis?"

"I don't know," I lied, not wanting to point the finger at my best friends, because I didn't want SeanMichael to form negative opinions about them.

"Now, do you honestly expect me to believe that?"

"Yes, because I don't have a reason to lie to you," I repeated.

"You must think I'm a fool," he retorted.

"Okay, well, you're going to believe whatever you want to believe. I told you I don't have a reason to lie. He showed up at my party uninvited and unannounced. When I saw him, I immediately asked him to leave."

"Did he give you a gift?"

Damn! This was so not a good idea.

"No. Russell has never given me anything but a broken heart," I lied, scared of what his reaction would be if I dared tell him Russell had given me diamond earrings that put his engagement ring to pure shame.

"He didn't give you anything?" SeanMichael asked a second time.

"I just told you no," I said, trying to sound more convincing.

"So why are you just now telling me that you've been seeing him?"

"I haven't been seeing him," I shot back in my defense.

"Y'all are partying together and whatnot. What do you call it?"

"I call it him trying to crash my party and getting kicked out."

"Yeah, right."

"What do you mean by that?" I snapped.

"I'm a million miles away, and I'm thinking you're there, being faithful to me. Then I find out your ex is coming around just whenever he feels like it, and you don't even tell me? You're making me not trust you."

"What!" Immediately I was pissed. "Are you accusing me of cheating? I choose to tell you what was going on with me, and this is how you react? I didn't have to tell you a damn thing! I could have kept all of this to myself."

"I would have found out some kind of way. What's done in the dark always come out in the light."

"I haven't done anything and don't appreciate you accusing me."

"And I don't appreciate you tiptoeing around with your ex-boyfriend. Did you screw him too?"

I gasped in shock, then started to cuss his ass out but got ahold of myself. "You know what, SeanMichael? I'm done talking to you. If you can't trust me, we don't need to be together. Bye."

"Oh, now you're ready—"

Before he could finish his sentence, I ended the call.

He called right back, and I pushed the ignore button, then turned my phone off for the rest of the night.

When I got home, I pulled his little rinky-dink ring off my finger and threw it on my dresser, where it was instantly hidden by the brilliance of those studs.

Chapter 27

Dina

"We're thinking about getting married in Paris," I shared with my girls. We were gathered around Candis' kitchen table devouring some Chinese food.

"Whaaat?" Candis dragged out the word. "All this time you've been crying that you weren't sure if you should marry him, and now, all of a sudden, you're getting married in Paris? Girl, I'm jealous!"

"We haven't fully decided if it will be there yet, but we were talking about it the other day."

"So are you sponsoring our tickets?" Celeste asked.

"You gotta ask Bertrand all that. He's the one with all the money," I answered

"I see! Trying to get married in Paris and so on. Lifestyles of the rich and—"

"But look, though," I interrupted, "I told you I lost my phone, right?"

"You haven't found that thing yet?" Celeste frowned.

"I think Bertrand has it."

They both looked at me.

"What do you mean?" Candis asked. "Like, has it and won't give it back?"

"Yep. I think he confiscated it."

"You probably just left it somewhere," Celeste suggested.

"No. I know exactly where I left it, in the house, in the kitchen. I know I did because I had to call Ms. Maybelle and let her know I was running a few minutes late for her appointment."

"So what happened? It was just gone when you went back to get it?" Celeste asked.

I explained how I sent Bertrand back to get it and how he claimed it was nowhere to be found.

"Yeah, he got that phone," she added.

"But it doesn't make sense for him to keep it," I pointed out. "Even if he wanted to go through it."

"He's going through all your stuff for sure. Just get a new one." Candis waved her hand. "Did you have insurance on it?"

"No, and I can't afford a new one."

"How the hell you gonna go to Paris and you can't afford to get a new cell phone?" Celeste asked with crinkled brows.

She found this hilarious, but I found no humor in it; it was the truth. She had a point, though, and I realized how ridiculous it sounded. If Bertrand could afford to spend ten grand on a destination wedding, then as his fiancée, I shouldn't have an issue with finances. At the same time, I still didn't feel comfortable asking Bertrand for money. It felt like I was giving up my independence. If he bought me a phone, then he'd probably feel like he had the right to go through it whenever he felt like it. I had nothing to hide, but I couldn't go for that.

"I could see him being curious and going through it, but why would he keep it, though? That doesn't make sense." Candis shook her head.

"'Cause Dina be ignoring his phone calls, and not calling him when she leaves the house and all that. You know how he is. He gotta keep tabs on her."

"Shut up, Celeste," I said, wincing. It sounded too much like the truth.

"He said if you ain't gonna call him, your ass ain't calling nobody!" Celeste laughed again.

We all did, but inside I was processing that thought. It was hard to admit, but that was what it felt like. Even though I knew exactly where I'd left my phone that day, I still looked all around the house for it, to no avail. I'd finally gotten out of the contract with my cell service provider, and I did not want to sign another contract just to get a free phone that didn't even need replacing. Bertrand just needed to give me my phone back. It had been three days; that was plenty of time to review my contacts, text messages, e-mails, and everything else. On top of that, who knew how many appointments I'd probably missed and all kinds of important business from people not wanting to leave a message? It was just inconvenient to be without my phone. I hadn't actually accused Bertrand of stealing my phone, but the more I thought about it, the more I was ready to ask him about it once I got home.

"Hey," I greeted, finding him in the kitchen, preparing some dinner. I picked up an apple and began munching on it, walked over to him, and pecked his cheek.

"Hey, honey. You hungry?"

"Where's my phone?" Dinner wasn't important to me right now. I leaned back against the counter and waited for an answer.

"What are you talking about?" He turned his attention away from the stove and looked to meet my eyes.

"I want to know what you did with my phone," I demanded, convinced that he had it.

"I don't have your phone!" he exclaimed, with an expression that suggested his innocence and that he thought I was crazy.

"I know I left it in the kitchen."

"Babe, I told you, when I looked in here, I didn't see it anywhere. I have no idea what you did with it."

We stared at each other for several seconds, not saying anything. It just didn't make sense that my phone would just dissolve into thin air. He had to have it. I'd just have to replace it.

"Well, I need a new phone. I haven't had my phone in three days, and I'm probably missing all kinds of calls. I don't want to sign a new contract, so I'm going to need about four hundred dollars."

Bertrand looked at me like I had just started speaking a foreign language. "Four hundred dollars, babe?"

"I don't want to go back under contract for another two years just to get a phone for free. I'd rather just replace the phone since it's been abducted by aliens or something."

"I'll just add you to my plan, then, and you can get a phone for free. We don't need to spend that money unnecessarily, especially if we're trying to go to Paris or somewhere."

I paused for a minute in thought. If Bertrand added me to his plan, I probably wouldn't have to pay a cell phone bill again, but he would be all in my business with tracking phone calls and ordering text message reports and stuff. I didn't have anything to hide, but I couldn't see myself just submitting myself to scrutiny like that. It just didn't feel right.

"Don't worry about it." I shook my head. "I'll just replace it."

"You don't need to do that. Just get on my plan. That resolves all issues. You'll have a new phone, you won't be under contract, and it won't cost anything."

Picking up the cordless phone in the kitchen, I refused his offer. "No, don't worry about it. Let me just call them."

While he stood sautéing pieces of chicken breast, I took a seat at the kitchen table. I called my service provider, did some negotiating for a better service plan, and agreed to a new contract in exchange for a new device. I hated that I had to do that, but I wasn't going to let Bertrand manipulate me with some hidden phone trick. He knew exactly where my phone was and didn't plan to give it back to me.

I happened to be off the next day and was home when the UPS guy brought my replacement, and within the hour I was up and running again. Coincidently, it wasn't even two days later when Bertrand came in the house after work, having magically found my phone.

"Look what I found sitting outside on the sidewalk right in front of the door." In his hand was my old device.

"Oh." I shrugged. It didn't make a difference at this point.

"So how did it get there?" I heard accusation in his tone of voice.

"Who knows?" I was busy reading status updates on Facebook and was less than interested. Candis and SeanMichael had a whole bunch of mushiness going on between their two profile walls that was a whole lot more interesting than this lie Bertrand was trying to sell me. I knew good and well, he didn't just find my phone lying outside in front of the door after almost a week.

"Nobody's been over here?" he asked, sounding like he was suggesting foul play on my part.

"Nope."

"I want to know how somebody knew it was your phone and to leave it on this doorstep."

"Because the somebody that's claiming he found it had it all along," I started to say but decided not to engage. It wasn't worth me even getting upset about.

He walked over to where I sat on the couch with my laptop and handed it to me. I took it without looking, dropped it on the chair, and kept doing what I'd been doing. In my peripheral, I could see Bertrand standing with his hands on his hips, like he was waiting for me to explain or react.

"What?" I asked after he didn't move after a minute.

"So who had your phone, Dina?"

"I don't know, and I don't care."

"You gotta know something," he insisted.

"All I know is I left the phone in the kitchen, and coincidently, you find it outside, after I replace it."

Seeing he was getting nowhere, he turned and left the room.

"Somebody left it outside the door, yeah, right," I uttered.

He stole my phone, plain and simple, and then tried to insult my intelligence by acting like he had nothing to do with its disappearance. What kind of fool did Bertrand take me for? *Skip Paris.* I could see right now this wasn't going to work out so good.

Chapter 28

Candis

It had been ten days since SeanMichael and I last talked, and I was determined that no matter how much I missed him, I wasn't going to make the first move, and I sure as hell wasn't apologizing. What I was doing, however, was watching the calendar, as I had determined that if I hadn't heard from him in two weeks' time, I was calling off the wedding. Obviously, he couldn't take me at my word and believe what I'd said, and I refused to put myself in a marriage situation where trust was not present.

SeanMichael finally did call on day eleven, and my heart did skip a beat, but I answered my phone nonchalantly, as if I didn't care if he'd called or not.

"Babe?"

"Yes," I answered, as if he were bothering me.

"This week's been hell without you."

"Mmm-hmm," I mumbled.

"How are you doing?"

"Fine," I blurted, keeping my answers short.

"Well. I've been thinking so much about you over the past few days, and I miss you."

Was he expecting me to say that I missed him too? It wasn't going to happen.

"What were you thinking?" I said instead.

"I was praying about our last conversation, and I know that I don't have any reason to not trust you. I got a little bit shaken because I can't be there with you, and I don't like that Russell has access to you and I don't."

"Me and Russell are through, SeanMichael. I've told you that."

"I know, babe, but I guess I can't help being jealous, because you're beautiful and I love you. No man wants the woman he loves to be sought after by another man."

"But I've already told you about Russell and that he doesn't want me. He's engaged."

"I just got a little confused with my feelings, babe. It's not you that I don't trust. It's Russell that I don't trust, but I took it out on you, and I'm sorry."

"SeanMichael, if I had something to hide, I would have never told you." That was why he would never find out about those earrings.

"I realized that after I thought about it, babe. I know you could have kept that whole thing to yourself, but you trusted me enough to share it with me, and in return I insulted you, instead of trusting you back and trusting you more. Please forgive me."

"You hurt me when you said what you said."

"I know I did, babe. I was just angry and frustrated, and I was wrong."

"So how do you expect me to be able to share my day with you if you're going accuse me and get mad about what I tell you?"

SeanMichael let out a pensive sigh. "I guess I wouldn't be able to expect much, and I don't want that kind of relationship where my wife can't share her day with me and is afraid to tell me what's going on. I reacted without thinking, babe. That's all. And I've been crazy out of mind thinking about you for the past few days, and just missing you from my life."

He was saying all the right things, and I liked it.

"If you will forgive me, I want to move forward with our wedding plans. I love you and need you, Candis. We've come too far to let somebody who means nothing tear apart what we've worked so hard at. It's nothing but the devil trying to fight us at the last minute, and I refuse to let him win, and the only way he can win is if you don't help me fight." He paused for a second, then asked, "Will you help me fight, Candis?"

"Can you trust me moving forward?" I asked, not wanting to give an immediate yes.

"Baby, I choose to trust you. I can't be there right now, but I choose to trust you, and I promise you, this will never happen again if you give me another chance."

I let a smile come through my voice. "You sure about that?"

"I'm positive. I can't live without you, and I don't want to try."

"Let's fight together, then," I finally said, accepting his apology.

"I love you, baby."

"I love you too," I said, reciprocating.

We stayed on the phone for another two hours, catching each other up on what we'd missed from not speaking in over a week, including new wedding ideas. When the call ended, I was excited that we were back together, but damn, I felt guilty about those studs.

Oh well. What SeanMichael didn't know wasn't going to kill him.

Chapter 29

Celeste

I couldn't believe Candis had us in the bridal store, trying on gowns. Even more I couldn't believe that she was actually planning to marry this dude. She was grinning like she was ten years old and it was Christmas morning when Dina came out of the dressing room in the dress she chose for us.

"It looks so good on you." Candis beamed as Dina pretended to glide down an imaginary aisle, holding an invisible man's arm with one hand and a bouquet of flowers that were just as invisible in the other. My stomach was turning flips at the site of this mess.

"Okay, Celeste! Your turn," Candis said, now smiling as big as she could at me. "Go put yours on."

I let out a sigh that I could no longer contain. This was beyond ridiculous, and I didn't have any extra money to be buying a dress for a wedding that probably wasn't going to take place.

"Candis, I really don't feel like pulling off my clothes today," I said. "Let's come back later."

"Celeste, go 'head," Dina ordered when Candis just stared at me.

I pressed my lips together and stood reluctantly.

"Why are you acting so nasty?" Candis asked, digging.

"I told you I don't feel like changing clothes."

"But you knew what we were coming to do when we left the house, Celeste. And you wait until we get all the way out here and now you want to show out."

"I'm not trying to show out, but please forgive me if I don't share your excitement about you marrying a man you don't know and never even met. Do you know how crazy that is?"

"It's my choice, and it's my life. What is it to you if I want to marry him?"

"What do you mean, what is it to me? You're my friend! I care about you!" I said louder than I meant to. Other customers looked over at us.

"If you were my friend, like you say you are, you'd be supporting my decision, Celeste, not fighting me every step of the way."

"Ain't nobody who is a real friend is going to really support you marrying a complete stranger." I shot my eyes over to Dina, hoping she would give some indication that she was in agreement. Instead she was preoccupied with her cell phone. "You are making a huge mistake, Candis, and the whole world knows it, so excuse me if I'm not jumping up and down about watching you ruin your life."

"Just because it's not what you would do doesn't mean it's the wrong choice for me. And you know what else? If you want something you've never had, you have to do something you've never done, and I'm doing just that. Seems like to me you ought to be taking lessons, seeing's how all you got is a jacked-up, jackleg buster of a man that you keep taking abuse from."

My mouth dropped open, but no words came out. I was stunned and insulted. "Screw you and this whole wedding!" It was weak, but that was what finally came out of my mouth. "I'll see y'all later."

"You ain't got to see me again ever," Candis shouted across the store as I made my way to the door and rushed out.

How was she going to be mad at me when she was the one fool enough to marry some guy she'd never even laid her actual eyes on, talking about he looked like Brian McKnight? She didn't know what he looked like. He could be using Brian's pictures that he pulled off the Internet and splattered all over his Facebook page. Candis was being a dummy, and she knew it.

I jumped in my car, started it up, and zipped through the lot, angry, frustrated, and hurt by Candis's words about my own love life. I didn't have a "real" man, but she didn't have to say that. I mean, everything I said was true. I wasn't really feeling this decision she was making, but she didn't have to go as far as she did with calling Equanto names.

The last place I wanted to go was home, knowing the kind of drama that was ever present within my four walls, but with nowhere else to go and no gas to waste, I found myself forced to be on my way there. As usual, I sat in the parking lot for a full hour, wishing I knew what it felt like to honestly love and be loved.

I started daydreaming about Keith, pretending that he was the love of my life. Really, in my imagination he was. I had grown fond of him during our morning break room interactions and often wished that there could be more between us. I didn't know how Keith felt about me, but in my fantasy world, he was in love with me and couldn't wait to see me every morning. I imagined him bringing me flowers and writing me little love notes and kissing me on the cheek.

We'd had a great time at Candis's party, and I couldn't remember a time I felt so good inside. I'd smiled and laughed so much that night, my cheeks hurt. He had a great listening ear and always showed me compassion whenever I shared with him some of the messy details of my life. He listened without judging and never made me feel foolish for still being married to Equanto, although I knew that one of the best things I could do for myself was divorce the man I'd haphazardly married.

If I wasn't married to Equanto, I probably would have tried to date Keith. As a matter of fact, I knew I would have. I wasn't sure how he would react, or if he was even remotely interested in me. Honestly, I was kinda glad that Equanto stood in the way of me finding out. Who knew what kind of fool I would make of myself by throwing myself at Keith's feet if I had the opportunity? I'd run the risk of him saying, "Celeste, I think you're a nice girl and an incredible person, but I just don't like you like that."

Damn! That hurt even in my imagination. I definitely couldn't take a blow like that in real life. Yeah. It was a good thing that I had a husband, as crazy as he was.

There was the one time when I told Keith about what had actually happened to my purse and a few other stories about how Equanto had gotten on my last nerve.

"Why do you let him treat you that way?" Keith asked as I sat across the table from him, sipping my coffee and nibbling on a prepackaged cheese Danish.

"What do you mean, let him? I can't control other people's behaviors," I said, unable to make my eyes meet his. I pretended to be distracted by a magazine, but I could feel his stare beating down on me.

"That's true. You can't control his behavior, but you can stop accepting it."

I was silent for a minute, thinking about his words, and realized I didn't know how to stop. "And how do you propose I do that?" I asked semi-sarcastically, because I didn't want to be transparent. It was easier to make him think my question was rhetorical. "What am I supposed to do? Just uproot my kids and leave, right?"

"I wouldn't say it quite like that. . . ."

"Then how would you say it, since you know what to do?" Out of nowhere, I started getting defensive and angry. I was tired of people having so many answers and ideas about what I should be doing, but when it was time to feed and take care of my boys, nobody could be found. Nobody had a damn thing to say. Nobody had an extra bed for us to sleep in, extra money in their checking accounts, or extra time to babysit. All anyone ever had any extra of was unsolicited advice. Keith probably meant well, but meaning well and providing help were two vastly different things.

Keith looked at me for about ten seconds, then stood and walked out without saying another word. I wanted to call him back and apologize, but I wasn't about to chase this man down. For what? He wasn't my man, he didn't know what he was talking about, and he couldn't tell me how to run or fix my life. I finished my coffee alone that morning, wanting not to care about what just happened. At the same time, though, his walking out hurt my feelings. We didn't talk for about two weeks after that, because I made sure not to go into the break room until it was about two minutes before I needed to be at my register. That way, I didn't have time to talk or get advice that I didn't want or need . . . or better said, that I just wasn't ready to hear, because the truth hurt.

It was because of an employee appreciation day, when the store brought in breakfast for the morning shift crew, that we awkwardly started up some dialogue. Chatting with him made me realize how much I'd missed him in that two-week time period, and I almost melted when he said to me, "Hey, you! I miss our little morning chats. You act like you don't have time for a brother anymore."

"I just had to make some changes to my morning routine, and they make me get here a little bit later than before."

"Yeah, I notice you rushing in at the last minute and getting right to work."

I nodded.

"Well, you know where I am every morning if you ever go back to your old schedule."

That very next day I was in the break room thirty minutes before my shift start time, just to be able to converse with my friend again. And in thinking about it, I wouldn't want to ruin it with a relationship. I'd just keep him as my fantasy boyfriend.

With a huge sigh I opened the car door and stepped out onto the pavement, forcing myself to go inside.

"'Bout time you got back. You know I gotta go to work," Equanto said, not looking up from the video game he was playing. The boys were in the room, playing, but came running out to greet me when they heard me come in.

"Hi, Mommy," they said in triplicate, gave me a hug, then went back to whatever they'd been doing.

"Okay, I'll take you." Most times he would easily agree to me taking him and picking him up. It was only when he was up to no good that he'd fight me over the keys.

"Naw, just give me the keys. I'll drive myself 'cause I'ma be gettin' off real late."

"E, don't start this up today."

"I'm taking the car," he said more adamantly, as if it would change my mind.

"You can drive the car, but you're taking me with you. Kids, come on. We're about to go somewhere," I called out to the boys.

"Stay your ass here, Celeste!" he growled, tossing the game controller to the side, leaping to his feet, and grabbing for my purse to get my keys.

"Y'all go get in the car," I instructed my sons.

"Why you always gotta be so damn contrary!" E said, still trying to get my purse from my arm. He was pulling and jerking me around the room, but I held on with all the strength that I had. The boys were moving too slowly, so I yelled at them to hurry up just as my purse strap broke.

"You ain't taking that car, Equanto!" I yelled, scrambling to get my purse back, but in an instant Equanto had dumped everything out of it and onto the floor. He grabbed the keys and pushed me aside, causing me to tumble over the arm of the couch, and headed out the door.

"Y'all gone back in the house," I heard him say to the kids.

"Get in the car, y'all," I screamed, rushing to regain my balance and get back on my feet.

By the time I got outside, the boys were climbing into the backseat and Equanto was plopping into the driver's seat. This was one of the times when weighing a hundred pounds less would have really come in handy. I could have actually run to the car, instead of doing the slow Fat Albert trot I was forced to do. And even that had me seriously out of breath by the time I made it to the passenger's side of the car and yanked the door open.

Even though my hand was on the car door handle and I was huffing and puffing for my life, standing between the open car door and the frame, Equanto shifted the car into gear and started backing up. Thank God he didn't put his foot on the gas. Just him putting the car in gear and taking his foot off the brake was enough to make me lose my footing and topple over. I was trying to hold on for dear life, one hand clutching the door and the other grasping for whatever I could get it on. Both my knees hit the asphalt, and holes were scraped in my pants.

"You ran over Mommy!" Quincy screamed. "Daddy, stop it! You ran over Mommy."

Equanto jammed his foot on the brakes, although the car hadn't moved very much at all, but the sudden stop jerked me forward and my head slammed against the bottom of the car's frame, and in an instant my head was pounding. Once the car was no longer in motion, Linwood jumped out and rushed to my side, trying to help me stand up, but his small frame could in no way offer me any help.

"You ain't . . . takin' . . . this damn car . . . Equanto," I panted, still on my knees and trying to pull myself into the car at the same time.

"Look how stupid you actin'," my husband yelled.

"Move back, Linwood," I huffed. I settled one foot solidly on the ground, and just as I started to push up, something in my chest felt like it exploded and forced me backward. I started gasping desperately for air, but I couldn't seem to get enough as an excruciating pain took over. I could hear my kids crying and screaming, and I saw Equanto's angry scowl looking down at me, but with every passing second they seemed to get more distant and fuzzier, until they faded into black silence, and I couldn't see or hear anything.

Chapter 30

Candis

I'd heard that there was always one girl in the bridal party that would show her behind, but I never thought it would be Celeste. I expected it to be one of my rowdy cousins, but not my girl Celeste. I had to run in the dressing room and cry for a few minutes to get myself together after what just happened. I knew that me marrying SeanMichael was unorthodox, to say the least, but I really thought my friends were supporting me.

Celeste didn't know SeanMichael like I did. I talked to him every day. I heard the sincerity in his voice. I snooped around on his page and did my own level of investigation. And there were some things that I found out that I didn't particularly like, but I thought they were tolerable and together we could have a happy life with each other.

SeanMichael was the nicest man I'd ever met. Well, not literally met, but the nicest man I'd ever come across. And forget whoever had whatever to say about it—I was going to marry him.

"You okay?" Dina asked, tapping on the door.

"I'm fine," I answered weakly. "I'll be out in a minute."

"Open the door, Candis," she ordered.

"No, that's all right. I'm coming."

"You don't need to be by yourself. Open this door," she said a bit more adamantly.

This time I did, although I didn't have the strength to look up at her. She came in the large stall and pushed the sliding lock to secure it behind her, then wrapped her arms around me.

I cried silently in her arms, overcome with an unfamiliar wave of emotion, then pushed back a little, looking directly at her.

"Are you laughing and talking about me behind my back, Dina?"

"Girl, no! I've already told you, if this is what you feel like you want to do, then I have to trust and believe that you are being smart and mature enough to make a decision that will work out in your favor. Even if it doesn't, you can always recover from it," she said, looking into my eyes.

"I don't want anybody in my wedding who is really not for me. I know that it sounds crazy, but I know that I'm doing the right thing. I prayed about it, I feel like God gave me an answer, and I have peace with it."

"I know you do, honey, and I am here to help you with whatever you need. I only have one life to live, and that's mine. I can't live your life and my life too. Judging from my own mistakes, I haven't figured out how to get things right yet, anyway, so how am I going to tell you what to do with yours?"

That was why I loved Dina. She knew how to stay in her lane. I did love Celeste. I just couldn't believe her today.

"Now, you know Celeste will eventually come around," she added.

"Don't mention her name to me." I jerked away from Dina and grabbed my purse off the bench. "Let's go."

"I'm just telling you because you need to be prepared to handle her when she comes to herself."

"I don't care when that is. If I see her again, it will be too soon."

"You know she only said what she said because she cares about you."

"So that means it's okay for her to have smiled in my face all this time and then showed out like she did today."

"If you think about it, Candis, Celeste didn't say anything different today than she did on the day you first told us. You know she's always felt apprehensive about SeanMichael, and honestly, we'd all be lying if we told you we didn't think it strange and unusual. You know that. You knew that when you told us."

Dina had a point. I did already know what people were thinking. That I was a fool. I guess I thought they'd had ample opportunity to voice their opinions and concerns and at this point they'd embraced the idea with me. Silly me. But at least now I knew what and who was dealing with.

"Let's go get something to eat," Dina suggested.

"No, let's go get a drink," I countered.

There was an Applebee's right up the street, so we stopped there and slid into a booth. After a few sips of a margarita, I did begin to feel a little better, although inside I was still angry. If I kicked Candis out of the wedding, it would upset my bridal party numbers, but I'd rather make that adjustment than have her pretending to be with me and calling me a fool behind my back. Or in my face.

As soon as I got home and out of Dina's presence, I called SeanMichael and told him what had happened. The more I talked, the louder and more animated I became, but SeanMichael didn't interrupt me a single time.

When I finally finished by telling him, "So she's out of the wedding," he said, "Don't worry about it, baby. If she is a true friend, she will come around, and if not, it's better that you know where she's coming from now rather than later. Just take a breath and release it. I don't want anyone upsetting my baby. We both know practically the whole world is against us, but I love God and I love you, and with that combination, ain't nothing gonna go wrong."

A smile crept across my face, like it usually did when I talked to SeanMichael. He always knew the words to say to make things right in my world. Now, instead of being angry with Celeste, I felt more disappointed that she wouldn't be included in the joy of my day. Celeste and I had been a part of each other's lives for so long, it would just seem weird that she wouldn't be around to help me celebrate the biggest day of my life. *Oh well. Life goes on.*

SeanMichael and I talked for another three hours, working through some wedding ideas and details. Since he was going to be flying out to Arizona, his selection of groomsmen was none, and I'd single-handedly picked out who would stand with him when he took me to be his lawfully wedded wife.

Chapter 31

Celeste

Feeling pain surge through my body, I tried to peel my eyes open, but they seemed to be held down with weights. So did the rest of my body. I could hear only a faint beeping noise, and then I felt someone rubbing on my right arm, which forced me to try a little harder to get my eyelids to part.

"Hey, sweetie," a familiar voice cooed.

"What are you doing here?" I asked, focusing my vision on my mom.

"Cain't no devil in hell keep me away from my baby when she needs me."

"Where am I at, Ma?" I said with slurred speech.

"In the hospital, baby." She ran her hand across my face. "You had a heart attack."

I eased my eyes back closed and let her words register. I was only thirty-one, and that was way too young for a heart attack. "Where's the boys, Ma?"

"Spending some time with Pop-Pop," she answered, referencing my dad.

Thank God for my parents. They lived in San Diego, which was pretty much a straight shot down I-8, but about six hours away by car.

"When did you and Dad get here?"

"You mean, when did you get here to San Diego?"

"I'm in California?"

"Me and your dad had you transferred here. You don't need to be out there with that monster you married."

I didn't comment, because my mom was right, and I was tired of defending Equanto, trying to find something good to say about him, when there wasn't anything good to say.

"Linwood told me what happened, and you know I had to talk your daddy out of killing that man. You do know that, right?"

I answered with a slight nod.

"I'ma go find a doctor or somebody to come in here and see how you're doing," she said, kissing my forehead, then leaving the room.

A heart attack? I couldn't believe it. All over trying to stop Equanto from what he probably ended up doing, anyway. What exactly it was, I'd probably never know. I had a lot to think about. I couldn't live like this. It was time to stop living for the hope that one day E would love me like I wanted to be loved. He'd never loved me. Never. And I'd been too unwilling to admit it to myself. I knew it, but I didn't want to accept it. I wanted to think that he found me to be enough. Good enough, pretty enough, intelligent enough . . . enough for him to love me. It just wasn't there and wasn't going to materialize out of thin air.

As I lay there, unable to even lift my head off the pillow, hot tears began to stream down the sides of my head and into my ears. How the hell did I get here? I questioned myself. Allowing my husband to steal from me, be an awful example in front of my three boys, destroy my self-esteem, and now put my life at risk. Granted, I was sure some of my having a heart attack was attributed to my weight, but me being constantly stressed out had to have something to do with it too.

"Thank you, Lord," I whispered, grateful that my life had been spared and I wasn't worse off than I was. I could barely move as it was, but at least I did wake up. That got me thinking how long I had been here. My mom said I was in San Diego, and since I didn't have any recollection of how I got there, I had no idea what day it was.

"The nurse'll be in here in a few minutes," my mom shared, easing back into the room.

"What day is it, Ma?"

"Sunday."

Sunday? The last time I remembered being conscious, it was Friday! I'd been knocked out for almost three days?

"Have the boys been up here?"

"Not yet."

I had mixed feelings about that. I didn't know how bad I might have looked, at the same time, suppose I had died and my boys hadn't seen me? Well, it didn't matter now. I wasn't dead, and I wanted to see my children.

"Can you ask Daddy to bring them up here?"

"Once the doctor clears you a little bit more, of course, baby."

I wondered if Candis and Dina knew where I was. Then I remembered Candis and I had had a bit of a falling-out when I last saw her. "And where's my cell phone?"

My mom rose from her seat and brought me my purse, then dug through it in front of me until she found my phone.

"Who are you trying to call?" she asked, checking. "It better not be Equanto Davis. I know that's your husband and all that, but I forbid you to call that man."

"Ma, please. Let me fight my own battles and have my own testimonies," I begged in a whisper. I knew my parents wanted only the best for me and had been devastated when I told them I'd jumped up and gotten married. And with them knowing some of our marriage issues, it didn't help in forming a positive impression of the man I'd married. "I just want to check my messages."

My mom dialed into my voice mail, then pressed the phone to my face. Of course, Candis and Dina had both called, sounding panicked and concerned. My job had called, wondering why I'd not reported to work. I smiled when I heard Keith's voice come through the receiver.

"Hey there. Are you all right? Haven't seen you in a coupla days."

Right after that I heard Equanto's voice start. I turned my head away, signaling my mom to take the phone and end the call. I didn't want to hear a single word Equanto had to say.

I was released from the hospital six days after I opened my eyes and realized where I was. I was still moving a little slow and decided to stay at my parents' house for a while, until I fully recuperated and got myself together. My mom and dad were glad to have me, and I'd never seen my boys look so happy and free. The sudden move impacted their school year, but kids moved all the time, and it probably wasn't that big of a deal, just a little bit of a hassle.

For the first time in a long time, I was able to really rest and not be bogged down with my usual messy life drama. I did miss Dina and Candis. They both had called to check on me, but each time was simply not an opportune time for me to talk with them. Besides that, I wasn't quite sure what to say to Candis, seeing as how last time I'd talked to her, the conversation wasn't pleasant. I owed her an apology, but I had to swallow some pride in order to give it.

I spent the first week just sitting in my old bedroom, thinking and crying about the decisions I'd made in my life, decisions that I regretted. As much as I loved my children, I hated the way Linwood was conceived, and because of my poor choices, he would probably never know his father. I regretted that I'd chosen Equanto as a mate and had two of his babies. I regretted that my sons were exposed to our fighting and arguing, Equanto's frequent disappearances and drama. I regretted finding comfort in food and eating myself to over three hundred pounds.

Keith's words kept coming back to me. "Why do you let him treat you that way?"

I wish I had an answer for myself. I wanted to say it was because it was what I had to do for the moment, but that wasn't true. I could have returned long ago to my parents' house if I'd needed to. I had to realize the power and strength I had in myself to walk away from a bad situation. Reaching over to my night table, I picked up my phone and sent Keith a text.

Hey you . . .

It was how he greeted me practically every morning.

Hey! How r u?!
Im better
Im glad to hear dat. Gettin some rest?
Trying to

> We miss u here in da store
> I miss being there
> U coming back soon?
> I don't no yet—gotta get some things worked out
> Understandable. U need N E thing?

That made me smile. I loved Keith; he was such a good friend.

> Just rest and prayers
> Other den dat—u ok?
> Yeah thx
> if u need me to take the boys out 4 a few hrs Id
> b glad 2. my daughter is here visiting
> dat mite b kinda hard—we in San Diego

Instead of my phone buzzing with a return text from Keith, it rang, displaying his number.

"Hey, you," I answered.

"Girl! What are you doing in California?" he asked in mock reprimand.

"I had to escape from all that heat, literally and figuratively." I chuckled.

"You have family out there?"

"Yeah, my parents. They are taking good care of me."

"I'm so glad to hear that, Celeste. You deserve for someone to take good care of you."

I wanted to say, "I wish it were you," but that was the totally wrong thing to let escape my lips.

"I'd do it in a heartbeat if I had the chance," he added and took my breath clean away.

"Boy, stop playing," I said, brushing his comment off.

"I'm serious, Celeste. I don't mean no disrespect when I say this, but your husband is a damn fool."

I didn't comment. It didn't feel right to agree with him, although I knew he was right. Keith telling me I was married to a fool made me feel like a fool for marrying him in the first place.

"I hate to see a man try to bring a good woman down, and that's what I see him doing to you. Tearing you down every chance he gets."

"Well, we're not together right now so I can get myself together."

"So you're going back once you get rested?"

"I mean . . ." I paused before trying to continue. "I don't—"

Keith cut me off. "You mean to tell me this joker done 'bout ran you over and dragged you down the street under the car and you haven't made a decision to leave his trifling, no-good ass alone?" This time Keith paused.

"I told you I have to work through some things," I said, trying to defend myself.

"Celeste. I pray that one day you wake up and look in the mirror and see yourself for the beautiful woman you are. I pray that you realize your worth and your value. Until you can do that, you're going to keep on taking his BS over and over again, until that man puts you in your grave. He almost succeeded this time, but thanks be to God you're still here."

While Keith spoke, I pinched my nose to keep from sniffing, not wanting him to know that I was crying.

"Wake up, sista. You got the power to turn your life around," he added. "You have my number if you need anything. I'll talk to you another time."

"Okay, Keith," was all I was able to utter. Even after the call ended, I stared at the phone in my hand for thirty minutes, replaying his words over and over again in my head while tears fell from my eyes and landed in my lap.

"I can do this," I said out loud to myself. "I can do this."

Chapter 32

Dina

While we'd kept up with Celeste via text, neither of us had seen her since the day at the bridal store. We both missed our friend and cleared our weekend to make the drive to San Diego to visit. Candis filled me in on the latest details of her wedding for a great part of the drive, which, after the first hour, I was sick of listening to. She was so excited about her pending nuptials, as any bride would be, me included if I was actually going to marry Bertrand, but I could no longer see myself doing that and being happy.

With the way things were right now, I was already on the verge of being completely miserable, and I just didn't see how sealing the deal with a marriage was going to fix anything. I felt myself slipping right back into the same pattern I'd been in when I was with Cameron, trying to accept and justify unacceptable behavior, including infidelity. I couldn't mess around and marry a cheater a second time, pretending like I had no idea. It just didn't feel like love to me, despite what came out of his mouth.

I pushed a stream of air from my mouth, thinking about the last argument we'd had over this very thing.

Even after Bertrand asked me what it was that he could do to earn my trust once again, and I told him, he'd not followed through. I'd asked him to clean up and throw out all his old relationship paraphernalia. Love letters, teddy bears, panties, cards, whatever. I wanted it all gone. Instead of complying and appeasing me, Bertand made excuses for why he couldn't do it, claiming it would take too much time, claiming that he had too much stuff to look through. I felt insulted and disrespected, to say the least. How could this man say he loved me and wanted to marry me, but then want to keep memories from relationships from times past? Was I not worth some "old" panties and love letters?

Then, looking at the type of man Celeste was married to, I felt a little silly complaining about things that seemed so minor in comparison to some of the stories Celeste shared with Candis and me. But still in my heart, it didn't feel right. Bertrand just didn't fit, and I wasn't willing to force myself to get used to it. I just couldn't see how Celeste had dealt with Equanto all these years.

I really hoped Celeste was okay and preparing her life for some major changes, even if it meant she'd be staying in San Diego with her parents instead of returning to her sorry excuse for a husband. I knew what it was like to really want to have a man, but I couldn't see being with someone who put me through as many things as she'd been through with Equanto—from his constant disappearing acts to him stealing her entire purse and throwing away vital records to make it look like a *real* robbery, not to mention the way he talked to her, calling her stupid, fat, good for nothing, and everything but a child of God. I knew only of a few times that they'd actually gotten physical, with him pushing and elbowing her, jacking her up against the wall, and craziness like that, but I knew the worst details of those times, Celeste kept to herself.

I felt bad for Celeste but tried not to judge her, because I hadn't taken a single step in her shoes. I didn't know what it was like to feel some sort of loyalty to a man because he was the father of my kids. I didn't know what it was like to feel guilty about taking those kids away from their father. Or to depend on an abusive man for a few dollars so that the kids could eat or could have lights and water. What I did know was Celeste didn't need that man in her life for any reason. He was nasty and manipulative, and I hated that Celeste had not only married him, but had chosen to stay with him.

Celeste had even told me about a time he'd brought a gun into their home and threatened to kill himself in front of her and the boys. I just couldn't imagine living under that kind of stress, control, and fear.

"We shouldn't go empty-handed," I mentioned to Candis, pulling into a Wal-Mart parking lot. "We can get a fruit basket and some flowers or something."

"If Celeste says anything stupid out her mouth today, I don't care if she's getting over a heart attack or not, she's gonna get dealt with." Candis pulled her purse up on her shoulder as we walked through the lot.

"Are you still mad at her? Girl, let it go!"

"I'm just saying. I'm not coming all the way out here to be insulted," she said, rolling her eyes.

"Candis, please take the chip off your shoulder. She's been through a lot."

"That doesn't mean she can just say anything she wants to."

"Just decide to be the bigger person," I suggested as we walked through the sliding doors and on to the produce department. "I doubt she's going to be in her usual snappy mood, anyway."

"Probably not, but still, you know how she can be."

Candis did have a point; Celeste was not one to bite her tongue.

"I'll go pick a card while you get the fruit." She walked off toward the stationery department, while I lifted prepackaged baskets of mixed fruits, looking for the best one.

"Lord, please don't let these women fight today," I prayed. Candis did act concerned when we heard about Equanto practically dragging her around the parking lot while she clung to the car, or something like that. All I could think about was James Byrd, Jr., that man that was dragged to his death in Jasper, Texas, behind a pickup truck in 1998. Celeste had said it was nothing like that, but she always played down Equanto's behaviors like it was really no big deal. I hated that she didn't take his meanness seriously.

"It wasn't really that bad," she'd say after she finished crying about him stealing her money, him slapping her in the face, him choking her over the car keys. "Trust me. He got some scratches and bruises too."

I didn't care how many scratches he walked away with from her trying to free herself from his grasp or defend herself. She was no match for a full-grown man, and Equanto didn't deserve her. As strongly as I felt, though, I was determined to keep my mouth shut about it today and to try to support her as best I could during our visit.

Chapter 33

Celeste

Dina and Candis tiptoed in the house, looking like they thought I was on my deathbed and they were scared to look at me. Nonetheless, I screamed with excitement when I saw them and opened my arms for a group hug. It was so good to see them both.

"Welcome to San Diego!"

Once they saw that I was actually fine and in a good mood, they dropped their apprehension and greeted me like normal.

"How're you doing, girl!" Dina asked, grinning.

"Good!" And this time I was telling the truth. I was good. I was well rested, was sleeping better, eating better, and had even dropped ten pounds since my heart attack.

"We brought you something," Candis said, thrusting a fruit basket my way with a smile.

"Thank you. This is about all I eat now."

"Yeah, I see your face looks a little bit thinner."

I didn't really believe Candis could see any weight difference, since I had so many pounds to go, but I thanked her for "noticing," anyway.

"Candis, I owe you an apology," I said before my pride could talk me out of it.

"I'm listening," she said, poking her lips forward with a half smile.

"I'm sorry, girl. I got some nerve trying to keep you from marrying your man and I got the raggediest marriage in the world," I admitted. "What does that song say? Sweep around your own back door before you try to sweep around mine, or something like that?"

"I know you meant well."

"Yeah, but I didn't have no business acting the way I did, or judging you or SeanMichael. Please forgive me."

"I'ma have to if I want you to be in my wedding," she said and grinned.

Chapter 34

Candis

I was so excited, I barely got a wink of sleep the night before I was finally going to meet SeanMichael in person. I'd spent the entire day before primping, just like I would if we were getting married as soon as he stepped foot off the plane. I got my hair done in Senegalese twists that fell midway down my back, got a full body exfoliation, a facial, and a manicure and pedicure. I also went to the makeup counter in the mall and had a young lady do my face and give me instructions on how to re-create the look so that I would knock Sean-Michael slam off his feet.

Instead of sleeping, I tossed and turned all night, dreaming all kinds of happy, romantic dreams, most of them taking place right in the airport. In one of the dreams, as soon as he got out of the Jetway and into the terminal, he dropped to a single knee and proposed. A preacher was there to officiate and marry us right on the spot, and we had a huge reception in the airport's food court. Now, the dropping to the knee, I could definitely go for, but our union was unorthodox enough as it was, so I didn't need to have the wedding at the airport to top it all off.

The morning of our meeting, I just wanted to relax my nerves as much as I could. I took a bath and took my time pulling on my clothes, bought especially for today's occasion. I chose a lavender chiffon sundress, which swirled around me every time I moved, like a flower being gently blown by the wind. I pinned my hair up in the front and adorned it with a large flower just above my ear that matched my dress, and then did my makeup. I looked stunning, if I did say so myself.

Dina and Celeste were due to arrive thirty minutes before I would leave for the airport to pick up a few things for our introductory dinner tonight. I was glad Celeste and I were able to circle around and get back to being friends, because I wouldn't have wanted to share the scheduled happenings of the next few days without her.

Right on time, they both showed up with trays and platters, ready to roll up their sleeves to prepare a few more entrees that would be taken over to my parents' home for our engagement dinner.

"You look amazing, girl," Dina complimented.

"Thank you!" I grinned. I felt amazing.

"You sure you don't want one of us to come with you, just in case he's some kinda undercover busta?" Celeste offered, having gotten back to her old self, except she wasn't with Equanto.

"No, my dad got this," I assured them both.

"All right then, girl. Go get your man," Celeste smiled.

"You ain't gotta tell me twice!" I did a circle snap, puckering my lips.

They walked me to the car, tucking in loose braids and making sure there was no lint on my clothes or lipstick on my teeth. We hugged at my car; then I got inside.

"I'll see y'all at my parents'."

"We'll be there!" they said in unison.

Every few seconds, the butterflies in my belly took off for a quick flight. Then they'd settle, only to take off again. I got to my parents' house in fifteen minutes and let myself in. My mom was scurrying around in the kitchen, preparing food, and Daddy was upstairs, probably still getting dressed.

"Look at my baby," Mom said, stopping her movement to show her approval of my look.

"I look all right?" I spun in a circle with a smile.

"You look like a beautiful spring day," she said. "I'm proud to call you my daughter."

"Thank you, Mommy." I blushed. "What is your husband up there doing?"

"You know he's as slow as a turtle crossing a country road," she answered, swatting at the air with a towel. "You did right getting here early."

"Well, he's got about twenty minutes to get it together," I said and laughed, taking a seat at the kitchen table and popping a strawberry into my mouth. "Do you need me to help you while I wait for him?"

"No, because you don't need to do nothing that's gonna mess that dress up. You look perfect, and we're gonna keep it like that."

"Celeste and Dina should be here in a little while to help with whatever's left. They're at my house right now, cooking a few more things."

"Yeah, we will let them do all the work." She opened the oven and took out four cake pans of almond-coconut layers. The aroma that filled my nostrils was so heavenly, I closed my eyes and inhaled as deeply as I could. My mom made the best cakes in Phoenix hands down.

"You sure you ready to meet this man looking like that? 'Cause he gonna wanna marry you sho'nuff with the way you looking." Daddy had sneaked downstairs and stood in the kitchen, dressed in perfectly creased gray slacks and a white oxford, crisp with starch from the cleaners. His sleeves were cuffed, creating a relaxed look, and a black belt circled his waist to match the black loafers he wore on his feet. His wavy hair was brushed down against his scalp, and a fresh shave had him sharper than a tack. My daddy was one smooth brother.

"Mom, look at Daddy, looking all fly and debonair."

"That's why I married him," she said, walking into his arms and meeting his lips with her own.

Daddy cupped her behind in his hands.

"All right now. Don't get nothing started that you ain't got time to finish," she said, giggling and pushing him away.

"Oh, I got time! We ain't got to meet the plane. We just need to pick him up."

"All right, Daddy. Time to go!" I said, jumping to my feet and wedging them apart.

"What you rushing for now?" he teased as he playfully pushed me away. "He done waited all this time. Another hour ain't gone kill 'im."

"I'm going to the car." I stood, grabbing my purse, keys, and few more strawberries. "Bye, Mom." When she didn't answer, I looked over my shoulder and saw that her mouth was full of my daddy's lips. "Come on, Daddy!"

"You just wait till I get back here," he warned my mom, pulling away and following me down the hallway leading to the front door.

I couldn't help but laugh at my parents, still keeping it hot after twenty-some years.

"So how are you feeling, baby girl?" Daddy asked me once we were settled in the car and on the highway.

"Nervous."

"A good nervous or a bad nervous? 'Cause you know you can just say the word and I will turn this car around and that joker can get back home the best way he can."

"A good nervous, Daddy, a good nervous. Keep driving," I instructed, pointing forward.

"All right now. I'm just checking, 'cause I ain't for no junk."

"That's why you're the best dad in the world," I responded, which made him smile like he did whenever I'd tell him that.

"Uh-huh. You're just saying that 'cause I'm your daddy, but feel free to say it as much as you'd like."

I felt like a little child waiting for Christmas Day to arrive as we sat at the baggage claim for Southwest Airlines, watching the flight arrival screens to make sure that SeanMichael's flight would land on time. It seemed to take forever, and I must have watched a million people walk by, examining every face that looked like it could possibly be his, although he had not texted me to let me know he'd landed yet. It wasn't until I went to the ladies' room, with my phone buried deep in my purse, my purse hanging on the back of the stall door, and me squatting over the toilet, releasing water, that my phone started ringing with SeanMichael's designated ring tone. Talk about Murphy's Law. By the time I dug my phone out, I'd missed the call, but I wasted no time dialing his number back.

"Hey, baby!" he greeted.

"Hey! You're here?"

"My feet are on the ground, well, not on the ground exactly. The plane is on the ground with me in it. We're taxiing to the concourse now. I guess I will see you in a few minutes."

"Yes, you will," I gushed. I checked the mirror and made sure I looked my absolute best, then rushed from the bathroom, as if he were already in the terminal. I was on pins and needles and couldn't keep myself from smiling if my life depended on it.

"He just called, Dad. He should be coming through in a few minutes," I blurted once I reached my daddy's side again.

"You ready?" he asked, throwing his arm around my shoulders.

"Yep."

Twenty more minutes went by before SeanMichael called and said he was approaching the baggage claim. I spotted SeanMichael weaving his way through the sea of travelers. As he got closer, I noticed his clothes were disheveled, and immediately embarrassment set in. He wore a dingy white polo that not only was in need of a hot iron, but also had what looked like a gravy stain splattered on the front. His pants were standard khakis that were also in need of ironing. They say clothes make the man, and if there were any truth to that, I couldn't rightfully say this was a man approaching me with a wide grin and open arms.

His hair was coiled in tiny knots so tight, it looked like he had a head full of stationary black bugs, and his shoes were a pair of sandals that looked like they had been borrowed from Moses, after they had been passed down through a few generations before they got to him. This was what he chose to look like to meet me for the very first time? I knew the flight from the East Coast to the desert was about six hours, but really, was that the best he could do? No one must have ever talked to him about making a first impression. Lawd!

"Hey, sweetheart!"

"Hey, SeanMichael!" I answered, still excited, but his appearance took away from the moment. I was truly taken aback.

He wrapped strong arms around me and pulled me close to him. At least he smelled good.

"Oh, my goodness, I can't believe I'm actually here with you," he whispered in my ear.

"Me either!" I replied, reciprocating.

"Thank you, Lord!" he said out loud, squeezing me extra tight. "Thank you."

We held the embrace for a good thirty seconds before pulling away.

"You are so beautiful," he commented, looking directly into my eyes. I could tell that in his world, for that moment, no one else existed besides me. "I love you."

"I love you too."

Our lips met in a kiss that was awkward for the first four seconds, while we got a feel of each other's mouths, then slid into a mesmerizing, intimate exchange of passion. After Daddy cleared his throat, we sheepishly broke away.

"SeanMichael, this is my dad, Ernest Turner."

"How are you doing, sir? SeanMichael Monroe," he greeted, slapping his hand into my dad's. "It's a privilege and an honor to meet you."

"Likewise, son," Daddy answered, scanning SeanMichael's choice of wardrobe.

"Oh, excuse my shirt. I, uh . . ." SeanMichael brushed at his clothes with his hands, as if the gesture would fix his appearance.

"Oh, don't worry about it, man. I know how it is to have to travel across the country. You want to be comfortable." Good ol' dad. He knew just what to say.

"Let me text Mom and let her know we'll be at the house in a few," I said, pulling out my phone. In all actuality, I texted my daddy, begging him to stop somewhere on the way to the house where SeanMichael could change into a decent shirt at least. I couldn't let anyone else meet him in the close to vagabond condition he was currently in. A few seconds later he texted back.

Leave that man alone

Daddy didn't understand. I was looking my best, and I wanted SeanMichael to look just as good as I did. Especially for meeting my entire family for the first time. Maybe he planned to change clothes once we got to my parents' house, which was where we'd arranged for him to stay until our wedding day. While Daddy went to get the car, we stood around the carousel, grinning at each other, holding hands, and nuzzling on each other, until finally his luggage came around, which was no more than an extra-large duffel bag.

"You ready, beautiful?" he asked as he heaved the bag up on his shoulder.

"Ready when you are," I chirped.

I didn't know how to tactfully ask if he planned on changing clothes or freshening up a bit once we got to the house. I tried to ease my way into that recommendation.

"You feeling okay? I know it was a long flight," I began.

"I was a little tired, but laying eyes on you and getting to hold you in my arms was the adrenaline shot I needed. I feel just fine, baby." He squeezed my hand tighter as we walked past a men's room. Couldn't he just shoot in there real quick, comb his hair, and change out of that god-awful shirt? Okay. It was looking like Mom would have to meet him as is, but I'd be doggone if he stayed that way all evening.

"I was just going to say, by the time we get to my mom and dad's, you will probably have about an hour and a half if you wanted to take a quick nap and change for dinner."

"Nah, I'm fine. It took me all this time to get here and be with you. I don't want to miss a minute of it sleeping. I can sleep after I make you my wife."

Inwardly I sighed. What was everybody gonna think looking at this sloppy man? I mean, I loved him beyond that, and would even help him to manage his image once we got married, but he couldn't fix himself up even a little bit?

Sure enough, when we got to my parents' home, after he hugged my mom, she showed him to the guest bedroom, and he put down his bag, then came right back into the living room and took a seat beside me. Obviously, he thought he looked just fine.

Mom had prepared chicken sandwiches, sliced cake, and iced tea, which we all ate, and we made small talk until SeanMichael asked for the floor.

"Well, Mr. and Mrs. Turner, I like to do things decently and in order, so first, I want to thank you for welcoming me into your beautiful home and allowing me to stay here during my visit."

"It's our pleasure," Mom answered. "We don't mind at all."

"I sure appreciate it," he said with a humble nod. "Now . . ." He stopped just long enough to clear his throat, then grabbed my hand, holding it in his own, and started again. "I know that my and Candis's relationship has had the most unusual start and has taken a path that has gained a lot of criticism and skepticism from a lot of people, and I'm sure you've had, and maybe still have, your own concerns. I want to assure you that I love Candis with every fiber of my being and have nothing but the absolute best intentions for her as an individual and for us as a couple. He paused momentarily and focused solely on my dad. "With that said, I'd like to ask your permission to marry your daughter."

Daddy let silence hang in the air for a half a minute while he gave a pensive stare. With puckered lips, he stroked the hairs on his chin, nodding slowly.

"You've spoken well, young man," Daddy finally began. "I do have my reservations, but I realize that my daughter is grown and she's always made smart decisions."

That was only because he had no idea of my string of relationship failures. Married men, abusive men, no-good men, baby-daddy men . . . But what Daddy didn't know wasn't gonna kill him.

"I'm gonna trust her, and the good Lord above, that you are the man she believes you to be, but I'm gonna let you know man to man, if you hurt my daughter, you won't live to hurt another living soul."

"I can understand and respect that, sir," SeanMichael reverentially answered.

"And it's with that understanding that my wife and I give you permission to marry our daughter."

A slow grin spread across SeanMichael's face. "Thank you, Mr. Turner. Thank you, Mrs. Turner. I am truly honored, blessed, and highly favored of God." He then turned to me. "Candis, you are the woman I've prayed about and prayed for, and I would be even more honored . . ." He paused as he slid from the chair and to one knee, digging in his pocket and pulling out a black velvet box, which made me grab at my chest and gasp. "If you would have me as your husband by taking my hand in marriage." He cracked the lid of the box to reveal a full-carat marquise-cut diamond set in white gold. It was the same one that I'd sent him a picture of that he said he couldn't afford. "Candis Lorraine Turner, will you marry me?"

From nowhere tears flooded my eyes. "Yes!" I exclaimed in a whisper.

SeanMichael took my left hand and twisted the ring he'd previously sent me off my finger, then replaced it with the new ring, which I just couldn't take my eyes off of. Somehow, I managed to stand up with wobbly knees, no longer caring about his stained shirt, his battered shoes, or his peasy head, and throw my arms around him.

"I love you, Candis," he told me again. And I knew in the bottom of my heart and in the depth of my soul that he meant it.

And just wait until Dina and Celeste saw my new ring!

Chapter 35

Dina

The day couldn't have gone more perfectly for Candis. While none of us could really speak to the kind of man SeanMichael truly was, we all saw how elated Candis was on her wedding day. We could only trust that Candis had sought God, received an answer, and had peace about taking his hand in marriage. Celeste and I were right there, supporting her, as she was given the royal treatment with hair, makeup, a fresh manicure and pedicure, and assisted into her gown. What a radiant and beautiful bride she made, and I couldn't have been happier for her. As I saw her come down the aisle to be joined with the man she loved, it did make me think of Bertrand and wish things had turned out better between us. But they hadn't.

Honestly, I envied her luck in finding true love and following her heart all the way to the altar, but my envy had its limitations. While every woman wanted to be in a stunning white gown and have everyone dote on her, especially the man she was committing her life to, I wasn't ready to marry Bertrand. No, I take that back. It wasn't that I wasn't ready. Bertrand was just not the right man for me. I'd never been one to support cohabitation, but living with him taught me the value of my own freedom and independence, and showed me just what kind of man Bertrand truly was. He indeed was all of the wonderful things that not just I, but other people, saw on the outside: he was nice, courteous, respectable, and a gentleman in many ways. However, underneath, he was controlling and didn't respect me as an adult. There had been many conversations between us where he'd in one way or another shown me that.

Celeste thought I was crazy, of course, not able to understand how I wouldn't just sit back and let a man take care of me. "Girl, I wish E would have gotten a job and said, 'Baby, you ain't gotta work. I'ma take care of everything.' He wouldn't have had to tell me twice. I woulda quit my job so quick, it woulda make his head spin."

That all sounded good, and Bertrand was willing to take care of me, but only to the degree that he wanted to. Only to the degree that he could control me. I had no say-so, voice, or opinion in things I felt couples should discuss and make decisions on. He would move only when he wanted to, and did only what he wanted, and when he wanted. And he never did agree to add that infidelity clause to that so-called prenuptial agreement he'd thrown in my face.

"How are you going to tell me what to do in my own house?" Bertrand had barked when I'd asked him a second time about throwing out his old stuff.

"It's disrespectful, Bertrand."

"I had a past before you, but I'm with you now."

"We all have a past, but still, don't you think the past needs to be cleaned up and done away with so we can start on a fresh and clean foundation? Instead of trying to build a marriage on layers of junk? I don't want to be finding somebody's old crusty panties and old love letters."

He blew me off and didn't even acknowledge what I'd said. Even after I poured my heart out and told him how much it bothered me, he didn't budge. He didn't move. And to me that meant he didn't care. It was definitely in my best interest to end things. I knew without a shadow of a doubt that I'd done the right thing in breaking our engagement and going my separate way. I could be nothing but extremely grateful that it didn't take me getting married first. While I didn't really believe that God had orchestrated a shacking situation for me, I was thankful that he had mercy on me through that time that I lived with Bertrand, and opened up my eyes to the things that I'd seen. Of course, Bertrand tried to convince me to stay and work things out, but I felt that his actions spoke louder than his words. His ego ruled his decision making, not what was logical or necessary for the betterment of our relationship.

Since Candis was going to be moving across the country with her new husband, she sublet her apartment to me, which spared me the probable failure of a credit check and forking over an application fee and a security deposit. She even paid up her rent two months out, which gave me a nice cushion for getting reset and reestablished on my own. I'd already transitioned my things from Bertrand's house, and not that surprisingly, he didn't put up any resistance to me calling things off and moving out.

"I still love you, Dina," he'd said when I gave him his key back.

I guess at the end of the day his love just wasn't enough to sustain a proper husband and wife relationship. The Kobe Bryant–size diamond ring wasn't enough. I'd wished him the best, given it back, and walked away with a clean heart and a clear mind. I'd have my day one day, but today was Candis's day, and I was happy to be her maid of honor instead of her matron of honor.

Chapter 36

Celeste

On our cues, we walked down the aisle ahead of Candis. Then she had her glorious moment in the sun, escorted by Mr. Turner. The wedding was as beautiful as any wedding could have been, and with applause, we all celebrated the couple, introduced for the first time as Mr. and Mrs. SeanMichael Monroe.

Now that I'd gotten over some of my own hurts and failures, I could really celebrate with her, instead of feeling a sense of jealousy for what I wished I'd had. Since I'd had my heart attack, as soon as I was able to, I'd committed to an exercise program. Whether I felt like it or not, rain or shine, I put my tennis shoes on and began doing better by my body by walking. It was hard at first, but before I knew it, I was up to five miles a day and enjoying every step. During those walks, I spent a lot of time in prayer, just thanking God for His mercy and His grace. I'd come to realize that my life was a precious gift from Him, and I was no longer going to waste it, but would live it to the fullest.

Each day I asked Him to help me with my eating choices so that I could get better and get healthy, and Him being the gentle and loving Father that He is, He answered my prayers. Instead of gravitating to the foods I'd always loved, I found myself loving new foods, unprocessed and healthy foods, fruits and vegetables and whole grains. Sometimes I did crave fried chicken and ice cream, and sometimes I treated myself to them, but food was no longer my source of comfort. I no longer tried to eat my way to happiness.

I found happiness in the fact that I was no longer living my life in danger. My children were no longer being exposed to unnecessary drama and a negative example of what a man should be. I thanked God continuously for my daddy, who was an excellent example for my boys, and while I was sure they missed Equanto just because he was, and would always be, their father—for my youngest two boys—my daddy left nothing lacking outside of the title of biological father. My boys were happier, healthier, and were even performing better in school. They even looked better physically.

As part of my total body healing, I'd also started seeing a professional counselor to help me realize and understand why I'd made poor relationship choices. Dr. Bell gave me exercises and thinking points that helped me to focus on the woman I was inside and to see myself in a positive and beautiful light. I'd done a lot of growing and still had a lot of growing to do, but I knew now that I was worthy of love. True love. Not a counterfeit love that belittled and tore down, but one that edified, encouraged, and supported.

I had kept in contact with Keith and had kept things platonic between us. I appreciated the fact that he had never disrespected or tested the boundaries that were around my marriage, but had always provided a listening ear when I needed one. He was the first person that I'd shared my divorce filings with, and while he didn't cheer like he was at the Super Bowl, he was relieved that I'd moved on.

Somewhere in my heart, I had to thank Equanto for doing all that he did, because through it all, I'd become a stronger and better person for it, and it showed. I was even five dress sizes smaller, having lost fifty pounds, and was no longer ashamed of myself and my life. God had been really good to me, and it felt so good to be free.

Chapter 37

Candis

Everything that I thought I wanted, I never really wanted those things. I wanted exactly what I had, a man who feared God, loved God, and loved me.

Today I married my friend, a man who loved me for me, regardless of my shortcomings, my flaws, my mistakes, and my mishaps. I knew everybody thought that I was crazy and I was being foolish, but what God had for me was for me. I guess there was such a thing as destiny and purpose, after all. The odds were against us, but the way I saw it, the odds were against every marriage. No marriage was going to be a sunshiny day every single day. There would be rain for sure, but knowing that God was on our side made every step of this journey worth it.

As SeanMichael held me in his arms and swayed me to Heatwave's "Always and Forever," I fell in love with him all over again. I never wanted to let him go, and I never would. He whispered all kinds of loving things in my ear during our dance. I found myself in tears when he shared that he'd taken the money he'd been saving for a car, decided to forego his cell phone, and made other cuts, including doing without an earlier trip to Phoenix, to be able to get me the ring I wanted.

"I love you, Candis," he whispered in my ear.

"I love you too, baby." We kissed all over again in the middle of the floor, with our reception guests watching, until the DJ broke us up by speaking into the mic.

"All right, all right, wait for the honeymoon," he teased, causing our guests to erupt in laughter.

While we reluctantly pulled away, Beyoncé's "Single Ladies" blared from the speakers.

"Okay, all you single ladies, it's time to come on out on the dance floor for the bouquet toss," the DJ announced.

From all corners of the room, various women, some whom I knew, and some whom I didn't, gathered in a bunch, preparing to catch a specially made bouquet for this particular part of the celebration. In the traditional fashion, I turned my back, counted to three, and tossed the bouquet over my head and into the crowd.

Turning to face them, I saw that a young lady who had come with one of my male cousins was jumping up and down, full of giggles, with the prize bouquet in her hand. It took only a few minutes before she got back to her seat and screamed out again, having found a pair of one-carat diamond stud earrings nestled inside the bouquet.

End

Notes

Notes